CASTAWAYS
#3

Isle Be
Seeing You

Don't get stranded!
Read all the books in the Castaways trilogy:

#1 Worst Class Trip Ever

#2 Weather's Here, Wish You Were Great

#3 Isle Be Seeing You

From Aladdin Paperbacks
Published by Simon & Schuster

CASTAWAYS
#3

Isle Be Seeing You

By

Sandy Beech

Aladdin Paperbacks
New York   London   Toronto   Sydney

ALADDIN PAPERBACKS
An imprint of Simon & Schuster Children's Publishing Division
1230 Avenue of the Americas, New York, NY 10020
Text copyright © 2005 by Catherine Hapka
Illustrations copyright © 2005 by Jimmy Holder
All rights reserved, including the right of reproduction in whole or in part in any form.
ALADDIN PAPERBACKS and colophon are registered trademarks of Simon & Schuster, Inc.
Designed by Tom Daly
The text of this book was set in Golden Cockerel.
Manufactured in the United States of America
First Aladdin Paperbacks edition August 2005
2 4 6 8 10 9 7 5 3 1
Library of Congress Control Number 2004109007
ISBN 0-689-87598-3

Isle Be
Seeing You

One

My parents have always told me that people can get used to just about anything. I used to be pretty skeptical about that, mostly because Mom and Dad were usually trying to convince me to "get used to" something I didn't want to get used to at all, like steamed broccoli or my little brother, Kenny.

But after being stranded on a deserted island with eight other middle-schoolers, the craziest teacher in school, and that very same obnoxious little brother, I'm starting to think maybe Mom and Dad were right all along.

Castaways

I found myself pondering that concept as I sat on the beach one sunny tropical morning trying to open a coconut with a screwdriver. I was wearing clothes that hadn't been washed in two weeks, every inch of exposed skin itched from my newest layer of sunburn and bug bites, and a jagged seashell was poking me in the butt. The weird part? It all felt almost normal.

"Come on, Dani." Chrissie Saunders broke into my deep thoughts with a weary sigh and a pouty look. She wriggled her toes in the sand and stared at me. "We're only trying to help."

"Yeah, really!" added her twin sister, Cassie, with all the melodrama she could muster. And she could muster quite a bit. Her big brown eyes widened, her lower lip quivered. Even her springy dark hair seemed to get a little springier. "If you don't figure out what to do about Josh soon, we'll just die!"

I sighed and stared down at the coconut in front of me. The twins might look all innocent and cute, with their big brown eyes and perfect light brown skin, but they could latch on like a pair of pretty little piranhas when they felt like it. Their constant nagging about Josh Gallagher was just one more thing I was getting used to after being shipwrecked on the sun-crisped little patch of sand, trees, and bugs we called Castaway Island.

You might be wondering how in the world a bunch of ordinary middle-schoolers from Florida wound up in such a bizarre situation. Good question. I mean, if one little thing, one decision or action or moment hadn't happened the way it did, everything could have turned out differently. I think that's what people call fate, but in this case, at least, it seemed more like the unfortunate result of a whole bunch of bad decisions.

Decision 1: My decision to sign up immediately for the environmental-cleanup trip that my science teacher, Mr. Truskey, was leading. Now, this was a bad decision because I already knew Mr. T was a little nuts. Whenever he's involved in something it goes wacky-doodle sooner or later. Usually sooner. Besides, I didn't even check with my best friends, Michelle and Tina, before I signed up, or find out who else was going. More on that when we get to . . .

Decision 2: Angela Barnes's decision to sign up for the trip too. Did you ever get a big old wad of used chewing gum stuck to the bottom of your shoe? Well, Angela is pretty much the chewing-gum wad on my shoe of life. And she likes me about as much as I like her, probably

because I'm just about the only one in the sixth grade who has the guts to point out that she's not nearly as perfect as she thinks she is. So when I found out she was signed up for the island trip, I decided I definitely wasn't going after all. Which leads us to . . .

Decision 3: My parents' decision not to let me back out of the trip. They claimed it was for my own benefit, but I have my doubts about that. Mainly because of Decision 3B, which was their decision to beg Mr. Truskey to take my eight-year-old brother, Kenny, along on the trip as well. I always thought they were joking around when they talked about shipping both of us off somewhere for a week or two so they could have the house to themselves. But apparently it was no joke.

Decision 4: Mr. Truskey's decision to eat a choo-choo bug. This was a big one. Like most people, I'd never even heard of a choo-choo bug—more officially known as the lesser equatorial beachwalker beetle—before the trip. That's because they only live on a handful of islands in the remote Esparcir chain. Within the first few hours on one of those islands, all of us on the trip got to know them way too well. They may be a rare and valuable part of the world's ecosystem, like Mr. Truskey says, but on

4

their home islands, they *are* the ecosystem. At least it can feel that way when four or five of the giant, ugly beetles are buzzing around your head while a couple more are nibbling on your ankles. So why did Mr. T decide to nibble back? Don't ask me. But like I said, it was a bad decision. Very, very bad.

Decision 5: I guess this one is another two-parter. Decision 5A would be when we all decided to board the boat that was supposed to take us back to the mainland despite the fact that Mr. Truskey seemed a little out of it. After he barfed up half his guts and passed out on the deck, we realized it must have been the choo-choo snack that did him in. That's when we moved on to 5B, which would be our decision to try to find our way back to the mainland on our own rather than dropping anchor and staying put until Mr. T woke up or someone found us. Honestly, 5B didn't seem like such a bad decision at the time. Who wants to sit around waiting for who-knows-how-long when there's any other choice? But it immediately became known as the worst decision of all time when our boat crash-landed on a coral reef and stranded us on yet another bug-infested strip of sand and palm trees.

So that's the short version. All those bad decisions had

led me to that moment, sitting on the beach cracking coconuts for lunch and talking about Josh.

Oh, yeah, about Josh. See, one of the things about Angela is that she feels like she's totally entitled to anything she wants. So when she set her beady blue eyes on Josh, I knew I had to intervene. He's such a nice guy that I was afraid he might not be able to recognize her true evilosity. After much thought I'd realized that the only surefire way to keep her from getting him was to get him myself—or at least distract him until we got rescued. That was when I'd gone to the twins for help, since they were the cutest girls in the sixth grade and generally had way more experience than I did with all things Boy.

"Well?" Chrissie demanded. "What do you think of our ideas? Are you going to try them?"

"Yeah," Cassie added. "Why aren't you even saying anything about this whole Josh situation anymore? You're acting so, like, quiet and thoughtful and stuff. It's totally not like you."

"Sorry," I said. "Guess I'm still a little tired from working so hard yesterday. You know, cleaning up from the hurricane and all." Two nights earlier a sudden tropical storm had attacked the island. Our little camp had been pretty

much totaled—our shelter, the fire pit, everything—
forcing us to spend the night in one of the bat-infested
caves in the cliffs lining the beach.

"Oh, yeah." Cassie wrinkled her nose. "My arms are still
aching from dragging all our stuff out of the lagoon. It
was worth it, though—everything's almost back to normal now."

Chrissie sighed loudly. "Whatever," she said. "In case
you guys didn't notice, Angela spent most of yesterday
following Josh around."

"I noticed." Cassie frowned at me. "She hardly did any
work at all. Unless you consider flirting work, like
Dani does."

I didn't answer, standing up and pretending to be very
busy picking out a new coconut from the pile nearby.
The twins were obviously getting kind of frustrated
with me, and I couldn't really blame them. They were
just doing what they'd promised—trying to help me get
Josh's attention.

There was just one problem. I already had it!

That was one thing I wasn't getting used to too
quickly. It still made me feel weird to think about it—
kind of light-headed and floaty, sort of like when I had

the flu. I could feel my cheeks going red and could only hope my sunburn hid the evidence of what I was thinking. Because no matter how much I was dying to tell the twins the truth about what had happened between Josh and me during the hurricane, I couldn't do it. Josh had asked me to keep it a secret. I still wasn't quite sure why, but I was trying to be understanding and accept his wishes. Wasn't that what a good girlfriend should do?

Luckily the twins started arguing with each other about which of them had done more work the day before and didn't notice that I'd fallen silent again. Sitting down beside them, I clenched my teeth as I struggled to pry open another coconut.

"Nice face, Dani," Chrissie teased as I grimaced over the coconut. "Really makes you look—"

"Hi."

I jumped, almost dropping the coconut on my own foot. Feeling my face starting to go beet red again, I looked up and saw Josh standing there.

"Hi, Josh!" Cassie said immediately, slipping into her talking-to-boys voice.

Personally I don't have a talking-to-boys voice. That's

probably because on a girlyness scale of one to ten, with ten being somebody like Marilyn Monroe and one being, say, Hulk Hogan, the twins rate about a nine and a half, while I'm probably closer to a three. Maybe a two.

"So, Josh." Chrissie smiled beguilingly at him, her eyes twinkling. "What's up? Were you looking for someone in particular? Someone like, oh, me, or Chrissie, or maybe *Dani*?"

I winced as Cassie giggled and poked her sister in the shoulder. They couldn't be less subtle if they were both wearing huge, blinking neon signs reading WINK WINK NUDGE NUDGE.

Josh scratched a bug bite on his tanned arm, staring at her uncertainly. "Um, I was looking for Dani." He pushed his dark hair out of his eyes and glanced at me. "You know that tent pole that got all bent out of shape in the storm? Ryan had a great idea—he turned it into a basketball hoop. We just finished hanging it up down at the far end of the beach. Want to come shoot some coconuts with us? We need one more to make the teams even."

"Sure," I said immediately. I dropped my coconut and screwdriver on the sand and stood up, ignoring the twins' dismayed expressions. I could almost read their

thoughts: *Alert! Alert! Jock talk in progress. Change subject to something girly, stat!*

"Okay, you guys," Chrissie said. "Josh, take it easy on Dani. Remember, she's just a *girl*. You know, delicate, sweet, sugar and spice, everything nice. . . ."

I rolled my eyes. The twins kept insisting I had to show Josh that I was more than just a girljock if I wanted him to notice me. Personally I thought that was stupid. Josh and I both played basketball—that was pretty much how we became friends in the first place. Why would he suddenly want to start talking about, I don't know, high-heeled shoes and nail polish? It totally didn't make sense.

"Come on, Josh." I decided it was time to get out of there before they embarrassed me any further. "Let's roll."

"Don't wander off together and get lost on your way there," Cassie said with a playful wink.

Josh looked confused. "Oh," he added. "Er, by the way, you guys can come along with us and play too if you want."

"No, thanks." Chrissie grinned at me. "I don't think Dani would like that very much."

"Have fun, you two!" Cassie trilled.

"Sorry about that," I muttered as Josh and I hurried

down the beach. It was midmorning, and the tropical sun was beating down with its usual enthusiasm. The sand was practically sizzling beneath my bare feet, though I hardly noticed. That was just one more thing I was getting used to on the island.

Josh glanced over his shoulder, his dark eyes puzzled. "Okay, do I have a big green booger hanging out of my nose or something? Because the twins were acting really weird just now."

I sighed, wishing I wasn't quite so honest. If I was sneaky and evil like Angela, I could just toss my hair and change the subject. Instead, I was going to have to tell him the embarrassing truth.

"They're, um, trying to set us up," I explained, trying to sound casual and matter-of-fact. In other words, *not* as if this whole conversation was making me totally uncomfortable. "I guess they think, you know, we would make a good couple or something. . . . You know they're obsessed with that kind of stuff."

"Oh." Josh ducked his head a little so I couldn't see his expression. But even so, I could tell he was uncomfortable too. Weirdly enough, that made me feel a little better about being so embarrassed myself.

"Anyway, don't worry," I added. "I didn't tell them anything."

"Oh, okay." Josh sounded uncertain.

I held my breath. Maybe he was changing his mind about keeping our new relationship a secret. Maybe he'd realized it would be easier to go ahead and tell everyone. Sure, it would be a little embarrassing at first. But at least everything would be out in the open. The twins would be happy for me, Angela would be miserable—it would be great.

Then Josh shrugged. "Okay, good," he said. "I was afraid maybe they'd figured it out or something."

My shoulders slumped. "Nope." I did my best to sound cheerful. "They're clueless. Totally."

We were nearing the far end of the beach by then, so we stopped talking. Up ahead a hilly wash of boulders and scrubby trees took over from the smooth white sand, tumbling straight down from the steep side of the island's central mountain into the clear, aquamarine water of the lagoon. On the flat section of beach on the near side of the rocky slope, four people were waiting for us. Ryan Rodriguez was attempting to juggle three coconuts while

Isle Be Seeing You

Brooke Hubbard looked on disapprovingly. Mr. T was twirling a chunk of his frizzed-out, overlong black hair around one finger and staring at the sky. Kenny was sitting on a boulder with his finger up his nose.

"She's in," Josh called out, jogging forward. "Dani's going to play."

"I call captain!" Ryan shouted, leaping about four feet into the air and waving his hand around like he was trying to flag down the space shuttle. For him, it was a subdued reaction. Ryan is what some of the teachers at school call *spirited*. Others just come right out and call him what he is, which is a total spaz.

"Me too," Brooke called out, raising her hand in a much more civilized manner. Everything Brooke does is civilized. As the only eighth grader on the trip, she considers herself much more mature than the rest of us sixth- and seventh-grade peons. She also considers herself a natural leader, probably because of her years of student council experience, so it was no surprise she'd called captain.

Josh shrugged. "Okay," he said. "Ry, go ahead, you get first pick since you called first."

I was expecting Ryan to pick Josh, who was clearly the best basketball player on the beach. Since I'm the

13

obvious second-best choice, if I do say so myself, I was already stepping toward Brooke when Ryan stabbed a finger in my direction and grinned.

"McFeeney," he announced, "you're with me."

Brooke may be a little too civilized for her own good, but she's no dummy. "I pick Josh," she called out quickly, as if afraid Ryan would realize his mistake and change his choice.

That left Kenny and Mr. Truskey. "Who should I pick?" Ryan asked me in a whisper.

I shrugged. Under the circumstances I didn't see much of a difference. It wasn't as if either of them was going to be much use on the court. Mr. Truskey seemed a little saner than usual at the moment—at least he was standing upright and focusing both his eyes on the same place—but choo-choo craziness aside, there was a reason he was a science teacher and not a gym teacher. He could hardly keep himself from tripping over his own Birkenstocks even at the best of times. Then again, Kenny was at least a foot shorter than anyone else, plus he was likely to get distracted at any moment and go chasing off after a choo-choo bug or something.

"I don't know. Mr. T, I guess."

Just then Kenny finally dragged his attention out of his own nostril and back to what was going on. "Hey," he said. "Pick me, Ryan. Pick me!"

Ryan shot him an apologetic smile. "Sorry, little dude. I'm going to have to go with Mr. T."

Mr. Truskey blinked and looked up from his own hair. "What did I win?" he asked happily.

"Looks like you're with us, Ken," Brooke said, sounding resigned. "Come on over."

Kenny stuck out his tongue at me as he skipped over to join his new teammates. "'S okay. I didn't want to be on *Danielle's* team anyway."

I rolled my eyes. Most people never call me by my full name, Danielle, because they know I hate it. Which is exactly why Kenny uses it as often as he can. "Come on, people," I said briskly, clapping my hands. "Let's get started!"

"Whoo-hoo!" Ryan shouted. "Come on, Mr. T. Let's huddle."

Mr. Truskey gazed at him. "What's that, Friedrich?"

Ever since eating that choo-choo bug, Mr. Truskey can't quite seem to keep our names straight. We were all getting used to answering to just about anything. I could only hope his choo-choo-addled mind still retained the rules of basketball.

"Just come on over here, Mr. T." I waved him over. "We'll explain everything."

Ryan insisted that I play center, which meant I found myself facing off against Josh. Mr. Truskey was assigned to guard Kenny, while Ryan raced over and positioned himself near Brooke, leaping and waggling his arms while she watched him with annoyance.

The game started. It was a little weird playing with a coconut instead of a real ball, as I discovered when I automatically tried to dribble around Josh as he came in for a steal. Feinting to the left, I pushed down on the "ball," already leaping forward to meet it on the bounce. The coconut plopped onto the sand and lay there inertly, and I felt my bare toe connect with it as I lurched forward.

"Oops." I felt my face go red as I windmilled my arms to stay upright.

Behind me I heard Brooke laugh. "Good one, Dani," she called sarcastically.

Josh grinned at me, but not in a mean way. "It's okay," he murmured. "I almost did that myself a second ago."

I smiled back. "Really?"

"Yeah."

I guess both of us sort of forgot what we were doing for a second. We just stood there grinning goofily at each other. I couldn't help noticing how cute he looked with a little bead of sweat dripping down his chin. . . .

"Yo! What are you guys doing?"

I snapped out of it and saw Ryan jogging toward us, looking perplexed—and maybe a little suspicious? Or was that just my guilty conscience imagining things?

Brooke narrowed her eyes. No question about it, she *definitely* looked suspicious. "Yeah, what's up, you two?" she asked. "Since when did this game turn into a staring contest?"

Oops. I winced, waiting for Kenny to start singing, "Dani and Josh, sittin' in a tree." But when I glanced his way, he was just standing there, not even paying attention to what was going on.

That wasn't like him. When it came to noticing embarrassing stuff about me, he was like a bloodhound on a scent. Humiliating me was the only thing he liked even better than collecting creepy crawly creatures and watching TV.

"You okay, twerp?" I demanded, a little worried about him for a second.

He just blinked and stared at me. I wasn't sure he'd even heard me.

"Is the game over?" Mr. Truskey wandered up to us. "Did I win?"

"We're still playing, Mr. T." Ryan stared from me to Josh and back again. "At least I thought we were. . . ."

Josh shot me a slightly panicky look, then opened his mouth. "Uh—I—we just . . . ," he began.

I stared at him, my stomach flip-flopping nervously, suddenly sure that this was it. He was going to blurt out the truth. It was about time—

"Hi, everyone!"

That voice. That prissy, sugary, totally irritating voice. I recognized it instantly.

Angela.

Just like that the tense, interesting moment was lost, scattered like sand in a hurricane by Evil Angela's untimely appearance. She strolled onto the court, ignoring my glare as she walked straight up to Josh, tossed back her shoulder-length blond hair, and smiled at him. Nobody believes me when I say she has evil powers, but it's true. How else could she spend so much time ship-wrecked on a deserted island and still look like she'd just stepped out of an air-conditioned mall after having her hair done and buying all new clothes?

"I heard you guys were playing basketball," she said. "So I thought I'd come down and cheer you on."

Josh shot me a nervous look and took a half step away. "Oh," he said. "Um, okay. Come on, you guys. What are we waiting for?"

Ryan clapped his hands. "Right!" he shouted. "Let's play ball, people!"

"Fine. Guys, I think I'll play center for a while," Brooke said to her team. "Josh, you guard Ryan instead."

I bent down and grabbed the coconut from the sand, resisting the urge to fling it straight at Angela's head. Why did she always have to show up at the worst possible moment?

We started playing again. But it wasn't much fun anymore. I managed to keep from trying to dribble the coconut again, but I couldn't keep from noticing Angela capering around on the sidelines. She hadn't been kidding when she'd announced she was going to be a cheerleader—she'd even picked up a couple of palm

fronds to use as pom-poms. The thing was, she seemed to be focusing all of her cheers on one person.

"One, two, three, four; come on, Josh, it's time to score!" Angela cheered loudly, waving the palm fronds over her head and doing a little kick. "Five, six, seven, eight; keep it up, you're doing great! Goooo, Josh!"

I gritted my teeth, tempted to march right over to her and tell her the truth. Josh didn't like her, he liked me. He'd told me so in the middle of that hurricane . . . right before he almost kissed me. (Angela interrupted that, too . . . grr!) I could almost picture the delicious, delightful look of horror on her face when she realized the truth.

Like I said, I was tempted. But I bit my tongue and kept quiet. Josh didn't want me to tell anyone, and so I was just going to have to keep quiet until he changed his mind.

What else could I do?

TWO

"Good game, everyone. Good game."
Ryan leaped around from one of us to the other, grabbing our hands, whether we offered them or not, and
shaking them enthusiastically. Mr. Truskey laughed and
shook back heartily, and Kenny added a high five when
Ryan got to him. Brooke and I rolled our eyes, but then
Josh started shaking hands with everyone too, so we
went along with it.

When Josh got to me, he stuck out his hand. "Good
game, Dani," he said loudly. As I took his hand he leaned

toward me a little. "Want to meet up in like fifteen minutes?" he whispered. "Butterfly spot?"

Angela was already making a beeline in our direction, so I just nodded. A shivery little thrill ran through me, as if someone had just injected carbonated soda into my veins. Maybe this secret-romance thing was sort of fun after all!

"Catch you guys later," I said to the group at large. Without waiting for an answer, I turned and loped off toward camp, doing my best not to wonder if the Evil One was already clinging to Josh's arm and batting her eyelashes in his general direction. What difference did it make? *She* wasn't the one he wanted to meet up with in fifteen minutes!

When I reached the camp area, Ned Campbell and Macy Walden were huddled together over the makeshift wooden table in the food-prep area, probably pulling together something for lunch. Macy was dressed in one of her usual *Little-House-on-the-Prairie* dresses, though the small palm frond she'd tied around her head as a visor added a touch of little-hut-on-the-island. Ned's fifth-degree sunburn was finally starting to morph into a tan, making his straight, bowl-cut blond hair look even paler

than usual. They didn't look up as I zipped past, and nobody else was in sight.

Inside the largest cave, which we used to store most of the luggage and supplies we'd salvaged from our sunken boat, I headed straight for the twins' bags. I knew there was a big, battery-powered light-up mirror in Cassie's makeup case, and she'd already told me I could use it anytime. Pulling it out, I switched it on and checked out my appearance. About half of my long, wavy, reddish-brown hair had come loose from its ponytail, leaving thin, frizzy tendrils flying in all directions. There was a streak of sand on my chin, and a dried leaf stuck in a clump of hair just above my left temple. Or maybe it was seaweed; I wasn't sure. In either case it didn't exactly scream "cool, sophisticated girlfriend," so I yanked it loose and tossed it aside. Realizing there was an easy way to clean myself up—not to mention get rid of any also-not-so-cool-and-sophisticated lingering sweat aroma—I dashed down the beach and quickly rinsed off in the surf.

Back in the cave, I quickly redid my ponytail, then turned my attention to my face. Staring dubiously at my high forehead, sharp chin, and turned-up nose, I tried to remember what the twins had taught me over the past few days about makeup tips and such. My head spun with visions of scented lip gloss, compact face powder, glitter eye shadow. . . .

"Whoa," I murmured out loud, shaking my head to banish the visions. "What's wrong with this picture?"

Switching off the light-up mirror, I sat back on my heels and stared at the cave wall. What was happening to me? Three days ago I was my regular old self—the same Dani McFeeney I had been for as long as I could remember. I was a normal person, a good basketball player, a loyal friend, and a decent student.

Then Josh had told me he liked me, and all of a sudden it was like I became a whole new person. A person who obsessed over how she looked and thought about glitter eye shadow and borrowed people's light-up makeup mirrors without a touch of irony. How had that happened?

It wasn't hard to figure out the answer. Everything since the hurricane had happened so fast that I hadn't really stopped to think about any of it. Now that I did, it all seemed weird. Some of it was good weird, like the actual Josh part. But the rest? Definitely weird weird.

You need to get a grip, McFeeney, I told myself sternly. Having a boyfriend is one thing. Morphing into some wacked-out,

Angela-type girly-girl because of it? Totally unacceptable.

I was slicking on a little Chap Stick when I heard foot-steps entering the cave. It was Kenny. "Hey," he said. "What are you doing?"

"None of your business." I quickly tossed the Chap Stick out of sight behind the stack of suitcases. It clat-tered against the rock wall, sounding awfully loud for a tiny bit of plastic filled with strawberry-flavored goo. I winced. If Kenny figured out what I was up to, I'd never hear the end of it. "What do you want?" I asked, mostly to distract him.

He shrugged and let out a loud sigh. "I don't know," he said, kicking at the stony cave floor with the toe of one grubby sneaker. The interior of the cave was dim, and it was hard to see his expression as I peered at him, but he already looked pretty distracted. "I've just been, like, thinking about stuff. Like my zoo, and the hurricane, and how you and Josh had to come rescue me . . ."

Did I forget to mention that part? The reason Josh and I ended up alone together during the hurricane was because of my brother. Kenny had spent a couple of days putting together what he called McFeeney's Magical World of Island Wildlife and what most people would

call "a disgusting collection of creatures only a professional exterminator could love." In other words, a bunch of bugs, toads, rodents, and lizards. This little zoo was located in a clearing about two-thirds of the way up the smallish mountain in the center of the island, and when the hurricane came howling down upon the island, what did my brilliant little brother decide to do? You got it— he took off up the mountain without telling anyone, determined to rescue his creepy crawlies from the storm. Josh and I wound up racing after him like a pair of demented marathon runners. We got lucky—the hurricane didn't drop a tree on our heads or wash us out to sea, and when we got back to the beach, Josh pulled me aside just long enough to tell me he liked me. Oh, yeah, and to almost give me my first real kiss. . . .

I sighed at the memory, momentarily forgetting about Kenny. Then he started mumbling again about whatever it was he was mumbling about, and I snapped back to the present.

". . . and I probably should have figured out about the storm and warned everybody, and—"

"Yeah, yeah. Whatever," I interrupted him in mid mumble. "Uh, I mean, that's okay. Nobody holds that against you or whatever. So you can chill." I was doing my best to hide my impatience. I could almost feel the seconds ticking away. Why hadn't I checked my watch back at the coconutball court? I had no idea when that fifteen minutes Josh had mentioned had started, or how much time I had left.

Then again, I couldn't help being a little worried about Kenny. He definitely wasn't acting like his usual obnoxious self at the moment. Thinking back to his earlier weird nonteasing behavior at the basketball game, I hoped he wasn't coming down with the same personality-altering choo-choo disease that had already struck Mr. Truskey.

"Hey," I said, interrupting him as he started to mumble again about his zoo and the storm. "You haven't eaten anything . . . weird lately, have you?"

He stared at me blankly. Then he smirked. "Yeah," he said, a little bit of the usual Kenny gleam returning to his eyes. "I ate that fried coconut you made for dinner last night. It tasted like roof shingles."

I rolled my eyes, not bothering to ask how he knew what roof shingles tasted like. I really didn't want to know. "Look, I have to go. Since you're such a food critic, why don't you go help Macy and Ned fix lunch?"

"Okay," Kenny said, sounding surprisingly agreeable. "Hey, Dani?"

"What?" My mind was already more than half out of there.

"Do you think we're ever going to get rescued?"

I stopped short, staring at him. "What?" I exclaimed. "Don't be a moron. Of course we're going to get rescued."

I didn't even bother going into detail. We all knew the drill. The second chaperone on the trip, Ms. Watson, had gone back to the mainland early with a sick kid. She'd probably started the search party about ten minutes after we didn't show up on time. It was just taking a while to find us, that was all. For one thing, thanks to our own stupidity (see Decision 5B above), we were probably miles and miles from where anyone expected us to be. In addition to that there was some kind of weird wind pattern over the Esparcir Islands that made it dangerous to fly a helicopter over most of the chain, so all the searching would have to be done via boat. When you considered that the hurricane had probably set things back at least a couple of days, it was no surprise that it was taking a while to track us down.

Isle Be Seeing You

But rescue was coming. No doubt about it. How could Kenny even question that? Did he think Ms. Watson, our parents, and everybody else was just going to give up on us?

Kenny shrugged. "Okay. Just wondering."

Rolling my eyes, I brushed past him and hurried out of the cave. Outside I squinted as my eyes readjusted to the bright sunlight. When I could see again, I checked my watch. It had stopped, probably because I'd forgotten to take it off earlier when I went for my morning swim in the lagoon. Oh well.

Deciding that a little early was better than a little late, I started walking briskly up the beach toward the jungle. My stomach was doing a funny little Mexican-jumping-bean sort of thing, kind of like it does after I eat a whole tub of popcorn and then go on the Rock-'n'-Roller Coaster three times in a row at the boardwalk back home. I took a few deep breaths as I walked, trying to calm myself down.

"Dani! Yo, wait up!"

Glancing over my shoulder in mid inhale, I saw Ryan waving wildly as he raced toward me. Swallowing a sigh, I turned and waited to see what he wanted, wondering if Josh might have sent him with a message or something.

Castaways

Ryan skidded to a stop in front of me, still all sweaty and red faced from the coconutball game. "Hey," he said, grinning. "What's up? You ran away pretty fast after the game."

I shrugged. "I guess."

"It was a good game, wasn't it? You were showing some pretty fancy moves out there." He danced around a little, pretending to fling an imaginary coconut toward an equally imaginary hoop. "If Mr. T hadn't accidentally passed the ball to Brooke like three times in a row, we might've won."

"Maybe next time," I said, trying to hide my impatience. "Listen, Ryan. I've got to—"

"Hey!" he interrupted. "I almost forgot to tell you. This morning I caught three of those fish you like so much."

"Fish?" I said blankly. "What fish?"

"Those reddish-colored ones. Don't you remember?" He leaned a little closer, peering into my face. "Yesterday at lunch you said they tasted better than the other kind. Anyway, I guess the hurricane must've stirred them up or something, because I barely had to put the hook in the water when *bam!* They were, like, practically fighting each other to grab the bait. . . ."

He rambled on eagerly for a few more minutes, punc-

tuating his fishing story with lots of fish imitations and other miscellaneous jumping around. I did my best to stay out of the way of his flailing limbs, wondering when he was going to shut up. Didn't he know I had somewhere important to be?

No, I reminded myself. He didn't. And I didn't want him to know either. So I just stood there, letting the seconds slide by and trying not to reach out and strangle him.

"Well, okay," I said when he finally paused for breath. "Lunch will be ready soon, so before then I guess I'll go and—"

"Oh! Speaking of lunch, did you notice anything funny about our chefs today?" Ryan waggled his eyebrows and grinned.

I glanced over my shoulder. Macy and Ned were still hard at work a little farther up the beach. Macy was standing at the food-prep table, her long brown braids almost touching the surface as she carefully sliced a papaya. Ned was nearby at the fire, stirring something that was cooking in a big pot. "Let me guess," I said wearily. "They're cooking that fish you were just talking about?"

"No!" Ryan exclaimed. "Well, I mean, yes. Probably. But that's not what I'm talking about. Didn't you notice that

Ned and Macy aren't even on the same work team?" He waggled his eyebrows again.

"Yeah, I guess." I shrugged, not sure what he was driving at and not really caring too much. A few days earlier, when it first became clear that we might be stuck on the island for a while, we'd divided ourselves into three work teams to make it easier to split up the chores. "Ned's on my team," I added. "We had meal duty yesterday."

"Exactly." Ryan smirked. "Now, you didn't hear it from me, but I think we might have a secret island romance brewing."

My heart stopped. I swear it did. "Wh-what?" I stammered.

Okay, maybe I should have seen where Ryan was going with his comments. It wasn't like he was being exactly subtle, what with all the eyebrow waggling and leading glances. But I was only half listening to him. Maybe not even half. So when he said the "secret island romance" thing, the first thing that popped into my head was me and Josh.

"Listen," I blurted out, instantly going on Full Panic Alert. "You can't tell anyone about this, okay? It's supposed to be a secret, and—"

Isle Be Seeing You

"You mean it's true?" Ryan sounded delighted. "Awesome! Yo, I was just messing around, mostly. Way to go, Neddie-boy!"

"Huh?" I stopped short in mid panic, belatedly rewinding the tape in my head. "What do you mean, 'way to go, Ned'?"

Ryan shrugged. "Don't you think it's kind of cool? Ned's barely ever even talked to a girl before, and now he's, like, totally hooking up with a seventh grader!"

"Oh." As the warm, comforting light of reality finally dawned on me, I sighed with relief. My secret was still safe. Better yet, maybe I could use Ryan's gossip to make my escape. "Hey, that is big news," I added brightly. "I don't know if it's true, but the twins probably do—you know how they keep up with that kind of stuff. I'm going to go check with them about it right now. Later!"

Not waiting around for an answer, I spun and sprinted toward the jungle. Even without a functioning watch, I was pretty sure I was way late meeting Josh by now. That couldn't be good. It wasn't that I thought he'd take off or freak out if I wasn't there exactly on time or anything. He wasn't that type of person. It was just that it seemed like a waste of precious time. Josh and I hadn't spent much time together since, you know, getting together. At least not without nine or ten other people hanging around. I might not be Romancina, Queen of Love, but I had the distinct feeling it wasn't supposed to be like that.

I sped down the path toward the stream, automatically hopping over gnarled roots and fallen branches along the way. About halfway to the spot where we all usually fetched water, I veered off the beaten trail and pushed my way through the underbrush, taking a shortcut through the jungle to a different trail, one we hadn't used as much.

Josh and I had never really discussed the "butterfly spot," but I had known exactly what he meant when he said it. We had run into each other there on our second day on the island, and Josh had pointed out a really cool butterfly resting nearby, all gauzy wings and vibrant colors.

I pushed my way through the moist, slightly prickly leaves of a cluster of shrubs. When I emerged on the other side, I stopped short in dismay. Josh was standing there on the narrow trail. But he wasn't alone.

"What are *you* doing here?" Angela and I asked each other at the same time.

Josh smiled uncertainly. "Hey, Dani," he said. "Um, what's up?"

Isle Be Seeing You

"Do you mind?" Angela added in a much less friendly tone. "Josh and I are trying to have a conversation here."

I glared at her. Once again I was tempted to blurt out the truth. *As a matter of fact, I do mind,* I would tell her loftily. *That's my boyfriend you're having a conversation with— isn't that right, Josh?* A tiny smile played around the corners of my mouth as I imagined her reaction.

I guess Josh noticed my expression, because he started to look worried. That reminded me that I had to control myself. At least a little.

"That's nice," I told Angela. "But Cassie and Macy are looking for you. You're supposed to be helping with lunch, remember? They sent me out here to get you."

For a second she looked confused. "What are you talking about?" she demanded. "Ned said he'd take lunch duty for me if I gave him the rest of my breakfast this morning. Don't tell me he backed out on me!"

Oops. "Uh, no, he didn't back out," I said quickly. "Er, I just don't think you should be allowed to do that. Trade jobs for stuff, I mean. It's not part of the rules."

"She has a point," Josh put in helpfully. "Maybe you should go back to the beach and take care of lunch, Angela. We can hold a meeting while we eat and decide

whether that sort of thing is allowed, and then you can work it out with Ned later."

I was impressed. Not only was that quick thinking, but he actually sounded all sincere and anxious about it. Nobody would ever guess he was just trying to ditch her—it really sounded like he was thinking only about the good of the tribe. Of course, knowing Josh, he probably *was* thinking about the good of the tribe. I just hoped that he was thinking about being alone with me too.

Either way, Angela wasn't buying it. "I have a better idea, Josh," she cooed, giving him her gooeyest, most look-how-cute-I-am smile. "This seems more like something we should handle in one of our leaders' meetings. So since Dani's here too"—she paused just long enough to give me a withering glance—"we might as well hold a meeting right now. We have tons of other stuff to discuss anyway."

"Like what?" I said. "We just held a leaders' meeting last night."

Remember what I was saying earlier about Brooke considering herself a natural leader? I forgot to mention that once we got stranded, we found out that her personal definition of *leader* matched up with our definition of *unbearable totalitarian despot.* That's why the rest of us rebelled, kicked her out of power, and decided to elect a new leader. Angela and I both campaigned hard for the position, but almost everyone else wound up voting for Josh instead. He agreed to accept the job, but only if the two of us signed on as his co-vice-leaders.

Angela smiled smugly at me and slipped her hand into the crook of Josh's arm. "That's okay, Dani," she said sweetly. "If you're too busy, Josh and I can hold a meeting ourselves and fill you in later."

Josh glanced down at Angela's hand on his arm, looking slightly dismayed. But he didn't make a move to shake her loose or tell her to keep her cooties to herself. And it only took me about 2.3 seconds to realize that the only thing worse than having Angela along on our "date" was having her on it without me.

"Fine," I muttered. "Let's hold a stupid meeting then."

As Angela started prattling away about something-or-other, I just stood there with my arms crossed over my chest, brooding. So far things with Josh weren't going the way I was expecting. Yes, he'd told me he liked me. Yes, we'd almost kissed—once. But was that really enough to be called a relationship?

Castaways

I had no idea. It wasn't as if I had a whole lot of experience in this area. The only thing I knew was that Josh wasn't ready to tell people about us yet, and I needed to support him in that until he came to his senses.

After all, wasn't that what a good girlfriend was supposed to do?

Three

"Take that, you stupid thing," I muttered through gritted teeth, hacking at the stubborn stem of a large palm frond. I only wished it was Angela's scrawny little neck.

The last few sinewy strands of fiber finally gave way to the dull blade of my knife, and the frond fluttered to the ground. Kicking it over toward the pile at the edge of the path, I swiped one arm across my sweaty face. My work group was in charge of shelter and latrines that day. Luckily the current latrine was still in pretty good shape, which meant we didn't have to dig a new one. But the

Castaways

strong sea breeze had ripped away some of the palm fronds that served as walls for our shelter, and it was our task to replace them. We'd already discovered that fresh, green fronds stayed put better and were less noisy than the dry ones that littered the ground all over the jungle, so I had volunteered to cut some new ones.

I glanced over my shoulder down the path. On my way out of camp I'd made sure to mention—loudly and several times—exactly where I was going, hoping Josh would hear about it and decide to track me down for another try at some alone time. Even while I was doing it, I already felt like the world's biggest dork. Or worse yet, the world's biggest Angela. But what choice did I have?

I looked around for another low-hanging frond, ready to hack out some more of my frustrations on the local flora. As I chopped away at my new victim, it crossed my mind that my parents probably wouldn't recognize me if they saw me attacking my chores with such enthusiasm. They're always saying I spend way more energy trying to talk my way out of chores than I would need if I just went ahead and did them in the first place. But it's really not the same thing at all. Once you've had to spend most of your time figuring out how to find enough to eat for

your next meal or where to dig yet another latrine because the old one's filled up, making the bed or emptying the dishwasher just isn't going to seem like a matter of life and death anymore.

While I was thinking about that, I heard footsteps crunching the fallen leaves behind me. I spun around, Josh's name already on my lips. Luckily it stayed there and didn't spill over into actual speech or anything, because instead of Josh, I saw my little brother coming toward me.

"Oh," I said. "What do you want?"

Kenny took a deep breath, looking earnest. "Listen, Dani," he said quickly. "Don't interrupt me this time, okay? I've been trying to tell you since the hurricane—I feel really bad about what happened. See, I should've figured out a storm was coming because of the way my animals were acting. If I'd told everybody, maybe it would've helped. Maybe the shelter wouldn't have got so busted up, and we wouldn't have lost those tarps, and . . . Well, anyway. I felt kind of, you know, dumb or guilty or whatever. Afterward."

I rolled my eyes. "Who do I look like . . . Dr. Freud?" I was honestly perplexed as to why he was telling me all

this. Kenny and I aren't exactly in the habit of sharing our deepest feelings with each other out of the blue. "What am I supposed to do about it?"

"That's what I'm trying to tell you, if you'll shut up and listen." He actually started to look sort of excited. "See, I think I figured out a way to make it up to everyone. I was up on the ridge fixing up my zoo yesterday. You know that other island you can see from up there? The close one?"

"Yeah. What about it?" From the ridge near the top of the mountain, if the weather was clear, it was possible to see several neighboring islands. Most of them were way off toward the horizon, but one was much closer, probably only about a mile or two away as the choo-choo bug flies.

"I guess the hurricane knocked down a bunch of big trees or something," Kenny said, "because there's a big gap there now, and you can see past that island to another one on the other side." He paused, staring at me as if trying to read whether his words were sinking in. "And I saw smoke coming from that one!"

My conscious mind had had enough experience with Kenny over the years to realize that most of what he said was an exaggeration or a delusion, if not an outright lie.

Isle Be Seeing You

I guess my subconscious hadn't gotten the message, though, because my stomach gave a nervous, excited little jump.

Then my conscious mind wrestled control back again. "Big whoop," I said. "There was tons of lightning in that storm—it probably started a forest fire or something."

He kicked at the ground excitedly, accidentally sending half my palm fronds into the bushes. "That's what I thought too," he said. "But I've been checking every time I go up there. The smoke is still there, and it's still in the same exact spot. I'm pretty sure it's from a campfire. There must be a tribe living there or something!"

I stared at him, not sure what to think. Was this part of some elaborate scheme to make me look stupid? It wouldn't be the first time. I winced as I suddenly remembered the time Kenny had convinced me that my favorite NBA player was doing an autograph-signing session in the ballroom of the local Holiday Inn. It wasn't until I found myself barging in on a meeting of the local nudist colony that I figured it out.

"Anyway," Kenny began eagerly, "I think if we—"

"Hey, McFeeneys!" Josh suddenly appeared on the trail, sending my already overwhelmed brain ping-ponging off in yet another direction. "What's going on?"

"Hi, Josh!" Kenny greeted the older boy. "I was just telling Dani—"

"Never mind," I interrupted, all thoughts of fire and Kenny and rescue and everything else fleeing to the back corners of my mind like roaches from the light. This was it! All I had to do was ditch my little brother, and Josh and I might finally get enough time alone together to figure out where we stood and what to do about it. "It's not important."

Kenny's face fell, and I felt a twinge of guilt. But I pushed it aside. I could deal with him later.

"Scram," I told Kenny. "We can talk about this later if you want. Josh and I have, uh, important leader business to discuss right now."

"But—," Kenny tried again.

"Go on!" I glared at him warningly. "I'll tell Josh what you told me, okay? But only if you leave us alone. Oh, and if you carry those palm fronds back to camp for me."

Kenny glanced from me to the pile of fronds and back again. His face shifted halfway into its stubborn, oh-yeah-make-me expression, but then he sighed. "Okay," he said meekly. Without another word he quickly gathered up the fronds and scurried back down along the path toward the beach.

Amazed, I started trying to remember the last time Kenny had done what I asked him to do without making a fuss. Then, realizing that was a waste of time, I turned and smiled uncertainly at Josh. "Um, hi," I said. "Want to go for a walk or something?"

"Sure." As we strolled deeper into the jungle, Josh glanced over his shoulder in the direction Kenny had gone. "So what was that all about?"

I sighed and waved one hand, as if trying to shoo the whole topic of my little brother out of our way. "Oh, nothing much. Kenny says he was up on the ridge and he spotted some smoke from another island." I shrugged. "I'm sure it's just a wildfire or something. Either that, or he's trying to lure me up there so he can feed me to his creepy crawlies."

"Hmm." Josh looked thoughtful, not even cracking a smile at my witty remark. "You're probably right."

I tilted my head, trying to read his expression. "What?"

Josh glanced at me and smiled sheepishly. "Oh, I don't know. I just wonder if maybe we should check it out. See, I've been thinking about ways we could, you know,

maybe get ourselves off the island. Just in case."

"Just in case what? Ms. Watson will find us eventually."

He shrugged. "I know. But we still don't know how long that will take, especially after that hurricane. That could really delay things, especially if it hit the mainland, too. It could be, like, weeks before they get their act together enough to really start searching again."

"I guess." Naturally it had already occurred to me that the hurricane couldn't have done our search party any favors. But somehow I'd been imagining the probable delay in days rather than weeks. Could Josh be right?

"Anyway, if there really is a tribe living on that island, that's big news. Huge." He smiled at me hopefully. "I know it's probably just a wildfire like you said. But maybe we should hike up there right now and see for sure—there's plenty of time before dinner."

I still had my doubts about Kenny's story, but the thought of a nice, private afternoon walk through the jungle with Josh made me decide to keep such thoughts to myself. "Okay," I said agreeably. "At least that way we'll know if there's anything to it before Kenny blabs to anyone else."

"Good point." Josh nodded. "Let's go."

Isle Be Seeing You

We were already heading in the right direction, so we just kept moving. The jungle was so humid it felt like we were walking through a car wash. Moisture slid from leaf to leaf and from leaf to ground in a steady drip-drip-drip chorus, harmonizing with the steady, soft hum of insects and the occasional familiar drone of a passing choo-choo bug. We came to a clearing—the hurricane had knocked down several large trees, leaving an open spot in the canopy that allowed the bright afternoon sunlight through, which instantly raised the air temperature by at least ten or fifteen degrees and changed it from a car wash to a steam bath. As we stepped back into the shade on the far side of the clearing, I felt something tickle my hand. I almost shook it off, thinking it was just another mosquito or choo-choo bug zeroing in on some nice human flesh. Just in time, though, I realized it was Josh. I let out a silent little sigh as I felt his hand slip into mine. This was more like it!

Still, I couldn't quite relax and enjoy it. I wondered if I should try to bring up the whole secrecy issue, or if it was better to wait and see if he mentioned it first. Before I could make up my mind, we both heard the sound of someone crashing down the path behind us.

Josh instantly dropped my hand, and we leaped apart. I almost crashed into a tree trunk but stopped myself just in time.

"Dani!" Ryan rounded the corner, breathless and sweaty faced. "There you are. Your brother said you were around here somewhere." He glanced at Josh, seeming surprised. "Oh, hey, dude," he added. "What are you doing out here?"

"Nothing." Josh shrugged. "Just out going for a run, and I ran into Dani."

I knew he was only trying to hide our secret, but it still felt kind of weird to hear him say that. Weird enough that for just a second, I was almost fed up enough to blurt out the truth then and there.

Then Ryan bent down, resting his hands on his knees to catch his breath, and Josh shot me a pleading, worried sort of glance. He looked so pitiful that I bit my tongue, feeling a little guilty for my irritated thoughts.

"Anyway, guess I'll keep going," Josh went on, his voice casual. "Want to get a couple of miles in before dinner."

Ryan's head was still down, so he didn't see Josh cast me another meaningful look and jerk his head in the direction of the ridge. Message sent and received. He was going up without me. I wanted to protest, but I reluctantly nodded instead.

"Okay, bro." Ryan finally straightened up, still unaware of the messages flying around over his head. "That's cool. I need to talk to Dani anyway."

Josh gave a little wave and then jogged off without a backward glance. I watched him disappear into the trees, feeling frustrated by my own bad luck. At least it wasn't Angela interrupting this time. . . .

Ryan was watching Josh leave too, but he looked a lot happier about it than I was. "Good, I'm glad he's gone." Realizing how that sounded, he laughed sheepishly. "Okay, sorry. It's not that I don't like the dude, I just have something I want to talk to you about, and it's kind of private. . . ."

I was barely listening. Maybe if I could ditch Ryan quickly enough, I could take a shortcut through the jungle and catch up to Josh before he reached the ridge. I scanned my mind for a good excuse.

Before I could come up with anything, Ryan mumbled a few words in Spanish, then took a deep breath. "Okay, here goes." His voice was suddenly serious. "Look, Dani,

Castaways

I could give you a whole big speech about your eyes and your hair and your smile and all that junk. But what I really want to say is this: Ever since we all got stuck on this island, I can't stop thinking about you and stuff."

Huh?

I snapped back to attention, my mind struggling to keep up with this totally unexpected turn of events. "What?" I blurted out.

He grabbed one of my hands in both of his. His palms felt clammy and warm. "I like you, Dani," he said as his face turned bright red. "I want you to, you know, be my girl!"

Four

To say that I was stunned would be the understatement of the year. My jaw dropped so hard it practically went subterranean.

"You wha—you wha—you huh?" I stammered stupidly.

Ryan grinned. "Hey, what can I say?" Aside from his bright red face, he seemed ridiculously unembarrassed by this whole conversation. "I have excellent taste in women."

I had no idea how to react. None. Nothing like this had ever happened to me before.

Ryan was smiling hopefully at me. The tiny part of my

mind that wasn't completely frozen in shock was telling me that I had to say something. But what?

This isn't fair, I told myself frantically. *I'm not the one who goes around flirting with boys and trying to get them to like me and stuff. That's the twins' department, or maybe Angela's. Anyway, I can't deal with this right now on top of everything else. I've just got to get rid of him.*

"Look, Ryan," I said briskly. "I . . ."

My voice trailed off as he gazed back at me, looking as happy and adoring and anxious as a new puppy at Christmas. How could I just blow him off? It was so totally what Angela would do. First a secret boyfriend and now this—was I turning into an Angela clone? Could the girly-girlness sneak up on you just like that, take you over, and turn you evil like her?

"Yes, Dani?" Ryan prompted me eagerly. "What do you think? Look, I know I didn't give you any warning. You don't have to decide anything right away. How about if we just, you know, go on a date or something? We could do a picnic up on the ridge maybe. What do you say?"

I opened my mouth and closed it a few times, my stomach sinking in my gut like a rock as I realized I'd just missed my chance to cut him off cleanly. It was as if I'd

been playing basketball, hoping to sink a shot, and ended up dribbling right past the basket, under the scoreboard, and out the gym doors into the parking lot.

Snapping my mouth shut, I smiled tightly. "Um," I mumbled intelligently. "Uh, let me think about it, okay?"

It seemed the best I could do under the circumstances. Unfortunately Ryan seemed thrilled.

"Cool!" he cried, his limbs twitching slightly as his grin stretched from ear to ear. Come to think of it, those few minutes during our conversation were the longest I'd seen him hold more-or-less still since arriving on the island. Or possibly ever. "Take all the time you need," he added. "You know where to find me when you make up your mind. See you, Dani! 'Bye! Catch you later!" The twitching turned into actual movement, and he danced off down the path.

I sighed as I watched him go. Okay. What was I supposed to do now?

An hour later I had made up my mind. I had to find Ryan and let him down easy. It wasn't fair to let him get his hopes up. It wasn't fair to me, either. Thanks to Ryan's little announcement, I'd totally missed yet another chance to spend time alone with Josh, and I didn't want that to happen again.

But finding Ryan was turning out to be harder than expected. He normally spent the afternoon fishing or bodysurfing, but that day there was no sign of him anywhere on the beach. "Hey," I said, sticking my head into the shelter. "Anybody in here?"

Brooke opened her eyes and looked up at me sleepily. "What?" she demanded. "Can't you see I'm trying to take a nap?"

"Sorry, I—"

A shout interrupted my response. Pulling my head out of the shelter, I saw Josh running down the beach waving his hands over his head.

Brooke sat up and rubbed her eyes. "What's all the yelling about now?" she mumbled grumpily.

"I'm not sure."

All over the beach, other people were looking over to see what was happening. Ned, who was reading one of the twins' fashion magazines in the shade of a palm tree, squinted curiously as Josh ran past him. The twins stopped splashing around in the surf and stared. Angela wandered out of the supply cave holding a beach towel.

Isle Be Seeing You

Macy glanced up from chopping something on the food-prep table. Even Ryan finally appeared at the edge of the jungle carrying an armload of firewood.

Josh raced over to the fire pit and jumped up on one of the logs we used as seats. "Hey, everyone!" he called. "Over here! I have something important to tell you."

We all drifted toward him. Since I was the closest to the fire pit other than Macy, I was one of the first to arrive. Josh grinned at me. "Guess what, Dani?" he exclaimed breathlessly. "Kenny was right! There's definitely a fire on that other island—and I don't think it's a wildfire, either. There's got to be people over there!"

"What?" Brooke was right behind me, still rubbing her eyes and yawning. But at Josh's words, she suddenly looked fully awake. "What did you say, Josh? Did you say you saw people?"

"Huh?" Cassie cried, running the last few steps to the fire pit. "Did someone say we're being rescued?"

"Rescued? What?"

All of a sudden everyone was talking at once. "Wait!" Josh waved his hands desperately over his head. "Listen!"

"Shut up, people!" I shouted helpfully. "Let him talk!"

Angela wrinkled her nose at me. "Gee, this is a first.

McFeeney the motormouth telling other people to shut up."

"Gee, Barnes the butthead acting like a total snot," I tossed back. "That's a first too. Only not."

I blushed slightly as I saw Josh shoot me a surprised glance. Normally I tried to control my Angela-insulting when he was around. I'm not sure why, since I'm usually quite proud of the wittiness and creativity of my barbs. But Josh is one of those people who's nice to everyone. I mean *everyone*—jocks, computer nerds, teachers, little kids, cranky old people, even Angela herself. It's one of the things that makes him who he is. I guess I was worried about what he'd think of me if he saw me at my most withering. Not that he was likely to have any delusions about how I felt about Angela. I mean, everyone who'd spent more than thirty seconds at Tweedale Middle School knew that Dani McFeeney + Angela Barnes = happy-happy-friendship-time.

The hubbub continued for a moment or two, but finally everyone quieted down except the twins, who couldn't quite seem to control their excited squealing. That was still quiet enough to allow Josh to continue.

"Anyway," he began, "I just ran up to the ridge, because of something Kenny—wait. Where's Ken?"

We all looked around for Kenny. I was a little surprised he wasn't right up there next to Josh doing a little victory dance. He isn't the type to be modest about taking credit for things; once after he got an A on his spelling test, Dad caught him on the phone with the editor of the local newspaper. He was trying to take out a full-page ad congratulating himself.

But my little brother was nowhere to be seen. "He's probably out trapping more helpless slugs and lizards for his zoo or something," I commented.

"Never mind." Brooke was staring at Josh intently. She hates being out of the loop. "Go on, Josh."

Josh explained what Kenny had seen, then what he'd just told me about going up there himself. "Anyway," he finished, his voice sounding sort of vibratey with excitement. "I watched the smoke for a while, and I'm almost positive it's a campfire."

"Wow." Brooke rubbed her hands together so rapidly I was afraid her palms might start to smoke. "Now that we know that other island is inhabited, maybe we should

think about trying to get ourselves rescued."

Josh nodded. "I've already been thinking about that," he said eagerly. "And I have the perfect plan. We can build a raft!"

"A raft?" Brooke sounded dubious. "Well, I guess that's one option."

Everyone else seemed equally underwhelmed by Josh's perfect plan. I guess it wasn't the reaction he had expected, because he looked surprised and slightly wounded.

"But wait." Cassie sounded a little confused. "Why are we even worrying about this? What difference does it make? Ms. Watson will probably find us any second now."

"Yeah," Macy put in quietly. "That's what we thought a week ago."

Josh nodded. "That's the point," he said. "We can keep waiting around for Ms. Watson, but there's no telling when she'll actually find us. So that's why I thought of a raft. We can take it over to that other island and ask the people over there for help. They probably have some way of contacting the mainland—they can tell the rescuers exactly where we are."

There was a moment of silence as everyone digested that. I'm sure I'm not the only one who was flashing back

to the pair of rough-and-ready rafts we'd used to transport our luggage and the other supplies from the wreckage of our boat. Josh and Ryan had thrown them together using a couple of wooden doors and some random bits of wood and twine.

"Come on," Josh urged, breaking the silence. "We can totally build a raft. We did it before, remember?"

"Yeah, but those rafts only had to make it across the lagoon." Brooke glanced out toward the glassy stretch of water nestled between the beach and the coral reef. "Going out into the open sea is probably going to be a whole different story."

"It's not really the open sea," Angela commented. "It's more like a channel."

"Thanks, Dictionario." I rolled my eyes.

The others ignored me. "I think Brooke is right," Ned spoke up. "It might not be the middle of the ocean, but there are waves out there. Serious waves. And currents. And maybe sharks . . ."

"Sharks?" Cassie cried, one hand flying to her mouth in horror. "I didn't even think of that!"

Josh flapped his hands as if waving away everyone's objections. "Okay, okay," he said. "I hear you. But listen,

Castaways

I'm not saying we should use those same rafts. Not even close. I'm saying we should build a bigger, better raft. An awesome, oceanworthy raft. The King of Rafts!"

I traded a skeptical glance with the twins. It's not that I didn't want to support Josh. It's just that I wasn't sure that floating off over the ocean on a raft—even the King of Rafts—sounded like the world's best idea. Sharks or no sharks.

Josh jumped off his log and crouched down in the sand. "Check it out," he said eagerly. "I'm thinking we use some of the tree branches that came down in the storm, and maybe the life vests we brought over from the boat. . . ."

He started sketching in the sand with his finger. The others moved closer, peering down at what he was doing. I watched too, hoping that Josh would draw something that would make me change my mind. But no. All I saw was a raft. The King of Rafts, maybe. But still a raft. And I had my doubts that any raft was going to carry us safely all the way to that other island.

Ryan scratched his head as he flung himself to his hands and knees beside Josh. "Hey, I guess that could work." Ryan is nothing if not an optimist. He stabbed

one finger at a particular spot on the drawing. "But I think we need better bracing there to counteract the blah blah blah...."

Okay, he didn't actually say "blah blah blah." But I had no idea what he did say, because all I could focus on at that moment was Angela, who stepped forward and leaned over Josh, resting one hand on his back. The nerve! I glared at her, wishing my eyes had laser-beam powers so I could shoot her straight off the island. Of course if I could actually do that, I could just shoot her right over to the mainland so she could tell the rescuers where we were, and then none of us would have to deal with this whole raft situation.

Since the laser-beam thing didn't seem to be happening, I moved forward a few steps, "accidentally" stepping on the back of one of Angela's sneakers. "Oops," I said sweetly when she yelped and jumped, almost tripping over Josh. "Sorry about that. I didn't see you there."

She glared at me, then leaned down to check her sneaker. One of her evil powers is the ability to keep every inch of her clothes looking clean, neat, and perfectly pressed at all times. That included her white sneakers—until now. Now there was a big grayish smudge on that heel, which gave me more satisfaction than it probably should have. But hey, when you're trapped on a deserted island, you have to take whatever kind of fun you can find.

Meanwhile the others weren't paying any attention to the two of us at all. They were all still staring down at Josh's neat sand sketch, which now had several messy Ryan lines added to it.

"I don't know." Brooke continued to look doubtful. "It seems pretty risky to me. And how do we know for sure that the islanders will even have a way of contacting the mainland?"

I started to nod my head in agreement. As much as I wanted to support Josh's plan, I wasn't sure it was such a great idea.

Then Angela spoke up. "Well, I think the raft sounds awesome," she declared, putting her hand on Josh's shoulder. She smiled at him. "You can count on me, Josh. I promise to work day and night by your side to help make it happen."

I stopped myself in mid nod, noticing the grateful look Josh was giving Angela. With a gulp, I quickly pasted a smile on my face.

"Me too," I said quickly. "I'm all about this plan. Totally."

Josh shot me a quick, extra-grateful smile. I forced myself to smile back, telling myself I wasn't really agreeing to the raft plan just because I was afraid Josh would start to like Angela instead of me if I didn't.

Even though I totally was.

Five

The next morning after breakfast

Brooke cornered me as I was washing papaya juice off my hands in the surf. I know, I know—you're probably thinking it sounds impossible to be *cornered* on a wide-open beach. But that's only because you don't know Brooke.

"Hey, Dani," she said, a funny little half-grin dancing around on her face. "I just talked to Ryan. So what are you going to do?"

I stared at her in horror. "He told you, too?"

The previous afternoon I'd been so distracted by the whole fire-raft-rescue situation that I'd sort of lost my nerve about the whole letting-Ryan-down-easy thing. So far I'd managed to avoid him, even though it was pretty obvious he kept trying to get me alone. Of course, at the rate he was telling people the whole stupid story, it wasn't going to matter soon whether we were alone or not. First Ned had grinned at me after dinner last night, muttering something about Ryan being a cool guy. Then I'd passed Macy on the path to the stream and found out Ryan had confided in her, too. At least Macy had some sympathy for my predicament since she knew about my plan to get together with Josh. Unfortunately she didn't know how that had really turned out—*secret* romance, remember?—so I guess she thought I should cut my losses and go for the sure thing.

"Ryan's really kind of sweet," she'd offered shyly. "I mean, Josh is great too. But you and Ryan seem more compatible, you know?"

Nice. Now the geekiest girl in the seventh grade was tactfully telling me I was aiming too high.

And now Brooke knew too. Delightful. Who was next—Angela? The very thought made my spleen quiver in horror.

Castaways

"Look, I don't want to talk about it." I pushed past Brooke. "So get off my case, okay?"

"What's the matter with you?" she demanded. "You don't have to act like such a drama queen; I'm just trying to make conversation."

Yeah, right. Trolling for gossip was more like it. But I couldn't really blame her for being surprised by my reaction. It wasn't like me to be all *no comment* about a simple question. Then again, it wasn't like me to have two boys liking me at the same time, especially since I couldn't even tell anyone the truth about one of them. That was kind of stressing me out.

Oh, and then there was The Raft. We'd started work on it right after that little meeting the afternoon before, and Josh and Angela were already out there lashing branches together by the time I woke up that morning.

Brooke was still staring at me expectantly. I knew she wanted to hear all the juicy details about Ryan, but I really, really didn't feel like discussing it with her or anyone else. It wasn't as if I'd *asked* him to start liking me. I wished he would just forget about the whole thing and go away. Why should I have to deal with something like that when I had so many other things on my mind?

Isle Be Seeing You

"I've got to go," I muttered in Brooke's general direction, not meeting her curious gaze. "I told Josh I'd find some more wood for the raft."

I headed along the beach toward the spot that had become Raft Construction Central. As I splashed through the surf I caught a sudden spasm of movement from up near the jungle. Glancing that way, I saw Kenny racing across the sand in my direction.

"Ugh," I moaned aloud, once again feeling trapped. When Kenny had finally turned up again the previous day, I'd been expecting him to get all gloaty-happy over the way Josh had followed up on his observation. Instead Kenny had seemed sort of agitated when he heard about the raft. Go figure. That would teach me to try to predict the reactions of my twerpy brother.

He'd found me a little while later as I returned from the latrine. "Dani," he'd blurted out without so much as a *hey-sis-how's-it-going*. "Did you tell Josh about the fire?"

"Yeah." Only about five percent of my attention was on Kenny. The rest was on Ryan, who was down near the water with Josh and the twins playing kickball with a coconut. "So?"

"You didn't tell him the rest of my plan to get rescued!"

Castaways

I rolled my eyes. "That's because you never told me, genius." I gulped as Ryan finally glanced over and spotted me. His face broke into an eager grin that didn't falter even when the coconut bonked him in the shin.

"Oh, yeah." Kenny didn't notice my distraction. "Anyway, Josh's raft idea will take way too long. My idea's better. See, I thought we could—"

Ryan was already jogging in my direction. "Sorry," I interrupted Kenny hastily, ready to sprint back into the woods. "Got to go. You can fill me in on your little plan some other time."

He'd been trying to do exactly that ever since. The trouble was, I didn't want to hear it. Okay, so maybe I still wasn't totally convinced that Josh's raft plan was going to work. But I wasn't about to let anyone know that—not when Angela was treating him like some kind of genius. Besides, how was some snot-nosed eight-year-old going to come up with a better plan than someone like Josh? I'd be ready to believe that about the same time I'd believe Angela Barnes was a decent person and not evil incarnate.

So that meant I had two people to avoid—Ryan and Kenny. Suddenly the island was starting to feel awfully small.

Isle Be Seeing You

"Dani!" Kenny cried now, waving at me as he barreled down the beach.

I suddenly felt an irresistible urge for a swim. Pretending not to notice Kenny's approach—or the fact that I was dressed in shorts and a T-shirt—I turned and splashed out through the tiny waves until I felt the firm, wet sand drop off beneath my feet. Making a more-or-less graceful swan dive into the deeper water, I swam straight out until I was pretty sure Kenny wouldn't come after me and then turned and paddled along the shoreline.

Macy and Ned looked surprised when I emerged from the surf like some kind of wacky shorts-and-T-shirt-wearing mermaid. They were the only ones at Raft Central; Ned was peeling the bark off a large tree branch while Macy picked at the knots and tangles in a big bunch of twine. The raft itself was already starting to take shape. Specifically, the big, rectangular shape of a bunch of sticks tied together.

"Hey, guys. Where's Josh?" I smoothed back my wet hair, trying not to feel silly about my impromptu swim.

Ned shrugged. "Haven't seen him in a while."

"I think he went into the woods to look for some bigger branches," Macy added in her soft voice.

"Oh, okay. Just wondering." I flopped down on the sand beside them, relieved at having escaped my little stalker—er, brother—once again. Not to mention successfully avoiding my spastic suitor for another few minutes at least.

I should have known it wouldn't be that easy. "Yo, Dani!"

I glanced over my shoulder, my stomach clenching as I saw Ryan hurrying toward me. "Oh," I said, my mind going blank. Now what was I supposed to do? "Um, hi."

"Hey, if you're not doing anything, can I talk to you for a minute? You know—privately."

Out of the corner of my eye, I was vaguely aware that Macy and Ned were glancing at each other knowingly. Feeling my face burn, I tried to maintain a normal expression, my eyes darting around looking for anywhere to land except on Ryan's eager face. I felt like one of Kenny's creepy crawlies trapped in one of his hand-made twig-and-pebble corrals. Maybe worse. At least the creepy crawly would have the comfort of knowing that a bird might fly down and chomp it at any second, putting it out of its misery.

"We can leave you two alone if you want." Ned was already climbing to his feet.

Macy nodded. "We need to go look for more twine anyway."

The two of them rushed off, leaving me alone with Ryan. Still sprawled on the sand, I stared up at him, feeling panicky and a little sick. This was it, then. The moment of truth. Or at least the moment of awkward, semitruth-based excuses.

He looked uncharacteristically serious. "I just thought we should talk. You know."

Suddenly salvation appeared at the edge of the jungle in the form of my little brother. Okay, that's not a phrase I ever thought I'd use. But sometimes you just have to go with the lesser of two evils. And seeing Kenny pop out of the trees and wave at me, I realized that escape was at hand.

"Sorry," I told Ryan, hopping to my feet. "Maybe later, okay? Kenny needs to talk to me right now. You know what they say—family first!"

I took off before he could respond, sprinting up the beach and skidding to a stop in front of my brother. Kenny looked startled at my dramatic arrival. Also a little suspicious.

"What's the matter with you?" he demanded.

"What do you mean?" I tried to shove him into the

shelter of the jungle, not wanting Ryan to get any bright ideas about following me. Glancing quickly over my shoulder, I saw him watching me. My sudden escape made me feel like a major dork, but I figured maybe in this case that was a good thing. It might make Ryan give up on this whole liking-me mistake. "Come on," I told Kenny urgently. "Let's go somewhere more private."

"You're acting like a freak." He flapped both hands at me to stop the shoving, hitting me in the stomach in the process. I was tempted to hit him back, but I could still practically feel Ryan's eyes boring into me. I settled for an evil smile.

"Okay," I said. "You wanted to talk to me. So talk. What's the big emergency?"

"You mean you're actually going to listen to me?" Kenny rolled his eyes dramatically. "It's a miracle."

"Very funny. Now talk already."

"Geeze, even when you're being nice, you act like a big jerk," he muttered. Then, seeing my glare, he quickly continued. "But anyway, I just wanted to finish what I was telling you yesterday. You know, about the smoke."

"What about it?" I was already losing interest. Another quick glance down the beach showed me that Ned and

Macy had returned to the raft. At the moment Macy was talking and gesturing in the general direction of the supply cave.

"You didn't stick around long enough to hear the most important part." Kenny's voice had taken on a sort of urgent whine that reminded me of the sound of a choo-choo bug in flight. "See, when I was looking at that smoke from the other island, I saw something else."

"Yeah? What?"

"A boat!" Kenny shot me a triumphant smile. "It was way out past that other island, like at the edge of the whole island chain, I think."

"A boat?" I repeated.

"Yeah. I watched again this morning at the same time, and I saw it again. I was thinking it's probably, like, a mail boat or some other kind of delivery thing that goes to some of the other islands every day, you know?"

"Hmm." Little bells of skepticism were going off in my head. This whole new boat twist seemed just a little too convenient to me. Chances were good that Kenny was making up the whole thing just to get everyone to pay more attention to him now that Josh had taken over the rescue plan.

"Yeah, right." I smirked, not willing to let him think he'd fooled me for even half a second. "Or maybe it's a big old cruise ship taking people on a daily choo-choo-spotting tour."

He scowled. "Don't be a dummy; I'm serious. If we want to get rescued, we should—"

I stopped listening. There was no room in my brain for Kenny's lame rescue plan, whatever it was. Every synapse was suddenly focused on Josh and Angela, who had just emerged from the jungle together a few yards away. She was clinging to his arm and laughing giddily. He looked uncomfortable, though maybe not quite uncomfortable enough for my taste.

My eyes narrowed as they reached Raft Central. Ryan, Ned, and Macy had wandered off again while I wasn't looking, so Angela and Josh were alone. But I didn't intend to leave them that way.

"Excuse me," I told Kenny. "I've got to go."

Six

If looks could kill, I would be nothing but a smoking pile of rubble on that beach right now. Because Angela sure wasn't happy to see me when I jogged over to join them.

"Watch out, Dani," she said prissily as I skidded to a stop in the sand at the edge of the raft. "Do you always have to be so clumsy? You just kicked sand all over Josh's raft."

"It's okay," Josh said lightly. "This raft has to survive a trip across the open sea. I think it'll probably be okay with a little extra sand."

I smiled weakly. Even though I was touched that Josh

was sticking up for me, his words pushed all my doubts about his raft plan to the front of my mind.

Doing my best to heave them off to the back again, I glanced down at the raft. "So what are you two working on?" I asked as brightly as I could manage.

"We were just about to start tying on some of the life jackets," Angela replied. "Why don't you run off and fetch us some more rope, Dani?"

I just smiled. She wasn't going to get rid of me that easily. "Looks like there's plenty of rope here already." I gestured at the sizable pile of rope, twine, and assorted spare shoelaces lying nearby.

"Actually, I just realized we should probably fix those rips in the life jackets first," Josh put in. "Hey, Angela, could you go get Macy's sewing kit from the supply cave?"

"Oh." Angela looked worried. I could almost see the evil little wheels in her mind turning. How was she going to get out of this one without revealing her true evilness to Josh? "Um, I'm not sure where it is. Maybe Dani could go find it instead."

I rolled my eyes. It didn't take a genius to notice that she was always trying to send out everyone else on little errands so that she could be alone with Josh. The girl was about as subtle as a choo-choo bug in a glass of ginger ale.

"How am I supposed to know where it is?" I demanded. "You're the one who organized the whole stupid supply cave when we got here, remember? While the rest of us were out in the hot sun carrying supplies and hauling water and building the fire and all the other actual work? Ring any bells?"

Angela scowled at me. But before she could respond, Josh put a hand on her arm. "Please, Angela?" He flashed her his most winning smile. "Dani's right, you're totally the best at finding things in there. Or maybe you could find Macy and ask her about it. I'm sure it won't take you long."

How could she say no to that? He'd asked so nicely, I was almost tempted to go on the errand myself after all.

"Well . . . okay." Angela returned Josh's smile. "I guess I can probably find it. Be right back." She hurried off in the direction of the caves.

When she was gone, Josh visibly relaxed. I only wished I could do the same. Yes, having Angela out of our hair for a few minutes was nice, but it didn't change the rest of my problems. Or rather, my one big problem: the secret part of my *secret* romance. If it wasn't for that, all my other problems would go away. Ryan would stop following me around, the twins would realize they could stop bugging me about Josh, and Angela . . .

"Wow, Angela's really excited about this whole raft thing," Josh commented with a smile. "I felt kind of bad sending her off like that when she's so eager to help. But I figured this was, like, a good chance for us to hang out a little bit, you know?"

I returned his smile weakly, not bothering to clue him in as to Angela's true motives. If he couldn't see it for himself, it would be too hard to explain. Besides, if I could convince him that the whole secrecy thing wasn't working, it wouldn't matter anymore. We could tell everyone the truth, and then Angela would probably shrivel up and blow out to sea from pure frustration and fury. The thought almost made me smile. Almost.

"Listen, Josh," I began tentatively. "I was thinking. You know how we decided to keep things a secret? About us, I mean. You know." I could feel myself blushing, as I always seemed to do when I tried to discuss that topic.

Josh looked a little embarrassed himself. "Yeah?"

"Well, I wonder if maybe—"

"Josh! Josh!"

I winced as Angela's familiar, irritating voice cut me off.

Glancing around, I saw her racing down the beach toward us, her blond hair flying in all directions and an excited look on her face.

As she reached us, she held up something in her left hand. "Check it out," she said breathlessly. "I just found this duct tape in the tool kit we brought over from the boat! I didn't even know it was there. We could use it for fixing the life jackets instead of having to sew them, couldn't we?"

Josh grinned, grabbing the roll of duct tape out of her hand and gazing at it as if it was the Holy Grail. "Yeah! Good eye, Angela. That will be awesome! It'll save us tons of time."

"You're welcome, Josh," Angela simpered, looking way too pleased with herself. "I'm totally glad to help."

You know how a bull usually reacts to a bullfighter's red cape? Well, that's just about the same reaction I always have to Angela acting self-satisfied. Sitting there and letting her bask in her own stupid glory wasn't an option, which meant I basically had two choices: I could say something, or I could leap forward and throttle her with my bare hands.

The second one sounded a lot more tempting, but I resisted the urge. Never let anyone tell you I have no

self-control. "Hey, I almost forgot," I blurted out, doing my best to sound normal and almost succeeding. Okay, maybe my voice came out a little squeakier and tighter than usual, but I don't think Josh noticed. "Kenny just told me he saw a boat going by."

Instantly Josh's attention was riveted on me again. "What? A boat? Really? Where?"

I was so busy basking in that attention that I almost forgot to answer. Angela's suspicious glare reminded me.

"Oh!" I said. "Um, I think he spotted it from the ridge. Out past that other island. Said he saw it yesterday and again today at about the same time."

"Wow!" Josh tossed the duct tape onto the half-built raft, his eyes gleaming. "That's incredible! Why didn't you tell us right away?"

"Yeah," Angela put in sourly, staring at me with suspicion written all over her face. "Why didn't you, Dani?"

I guess Josh, at least, meant that as a rhetorical question, because he didn't wait for an answer before adding, "This is awesome!"

He stared into space, looking excited. I guess either he was dreaming of being rescued, or he has an invisible friend.

Isle Be Seeing You

"Don't get too excited yet, Josh," Angela warned, still glaring at me. "It's not like this information comes from the most reliable source."

I wasn't sure if she was referring to me, Kenny, or both. I made an ugly face at her. Either way, I figured that should cover it.

Josh was still staring into space and didn't notice. "I'll check it out myself," he told Angela absently. "If it's true, this will make things easier. We can aim our raft at that boat instead of the other island!"

I gulped, forgetting all about Angela for a second. Even though I still wasn't sure whether Kenny's story was for real or not, I'd sort of figured that if it was true, it meant we could abandon the whole questionable raft plan completely and just figure out an easier and less shark-involving way to communicate with that boat. But now it sounded as though that hadn't even occurred to Josh.

"Ooh, you're so smart, Josh!" Angela cooed. Her voice had instantly shifted from harshly incredulous to gooey sweet and smarmy. "That's an awesome idea."

Yeah, right. I was pretty sure she would insist it was a brilliant idea if Josh suggested we all stand on our heads and sing sea shanties to help rescuers find us. That's the kind of person she is, and it's just one more way in which we're complete opposites. I always speak my mind, no matter what anyone else thinks of me.

I was just opening my mouth to do so when Angela spoke again. "Josh, we're all sooo lucky to have you on this island. Thanks for being such a great leader!"

With that, she flung herself toward him and grabbed him in a tight hug. Think big, blond leech attaching itself to human flesh.

Josh looked startled and embarrassed at the sudden display of affection. But he neglected to do what I would have done under the same circumstances, which probably would have involved an elbow to the throat. At the very least. Instead he gingerly patted her on the back as she clung to him. He also shot me an apologetic glance.

Realizing my mouth was still hanging open, I snapped it shut. Okay, so maybe when I said I "always" speak my mind, that was a tiny bit of an exaggeration. Because just at that moment, telling Josh my true opinions about his raft plan didn't seem like the best idea in the world. The last thing I wanted to do was make him mad and ruin our new, still uncertain relationship. Especially with Evil Angela hanging all over him, ready

to swoop in and take my place at a moment's notice . . .

Not for the first time, I found myself wondering uneasily what Josh really thought about Angela. Like I said, he's nice to everyone, so all along I'd been assuming he was just faking it with her. But what if that wasn't the case at all? A lot of people—especially boys—seemed to be taken in by Angela's insincere smiles, her pretty blond hair and nice clothes and perfect makeup. What if Josh—gulp—*liked* her, at least a little?

That reminded me about what had happened in those first couple of days on the island. Remember that election I mentioned earlier? Well, like I said, Josh won by a landslide. But Angela and I had each ended up with one vote in addition to our votes for ourselves. All along I'd been assuming that Kenny had dredged up enough family loyalty to vote for me. I was also pretty sure that Josh hadn't voted for himself—he had looked way too surprised when his name started turning up on the voting chips. That turned it into one of those logic problems my math teacher loved to give us. If Josh hadn't voted for himself and he hadn't voted for me, that left only one option. One that I didn't even like to think about.

I swallowed down my doubts about the raft along with

the lump that had just formed in my throat. "Yeah," I said weakly as Angela finally loosened her grip on Josh and backed away. "That should be cool."

It wasn't exactly the most enthusiastic endorsement in the world. But it still made me feel like a big phony. Not to mention a major wimp. Since when was I afraid to tell someone what I really thought?

But this was different, I reminded myself uneasily. Wasn't it?

"What is it, Dani?" Cassie asked as she followed me down the narrow jungle path. "What's the big emergency?"

"Yeah." Chrissie was right behind her sister. "Spill it. And this better not be just something lame, like Angela looked at you funny or whatever."

Reaching a small clearing, I turned around and stared at the twins, tempted to tell them the truth, the whole truth, and nothing but the truth. Unfortunately that wasn't an option, which suddenly made me feel lonely and kind of homesick.

A quick glance around confirmed that we were alone in that part of the jungle. I took a deep breath. "Have you guys heard about Ryan?"

"What about him?" Chrissie shrugged. "We've heard he's a spaz, if that's what you mean."

Cassie giggled. "Yeah. We also heard he looks kind of cute with his hair growing all long and his nose all sunburned."

"No, he doesn't." Chrissie wrinkled her nose distastefully.

"Yes, he does."

I rolled my eyes. The twins could turn just about anything into an argument. Just that day at lunch they'd spent about twenty minutes arguing over which one of them had more choo-choo bites on her legs.

"Listen," I said loudly, hoping to head them off before they really got rolling. "Ryan told me he likes me."

That got their attention. "What?" Chrissie demanded. "You mean, like, *like*-like?"

"Tell us everything!" Cassie ordered.

I sighed. "It happened yesterday afternoon. He just sort of came up to me and was all, I like you, be my girl, let's go on a picnic."

"You know, I sort of thought he was acting weird around you lately," Chrissie mused. "He was looking over at you a lot during breakfast. I kept checking to see if you had papaya on your face or something."

Castaways

"But wait," Cassie said. "What does this mean? Do you like him back, Dani?"

"No!" I shook my head violently. "No way. I mean, he's nice and all. But I don't like him that way. At all."

"Duh." Chrissie glared at her twin. "Get with the program. Dani likes Josh, remember?"

I winced. As far as the twins were supposed to know, I was just trying to be a good friend by saving Josh from Angela. Of course, they'd seemed a little skeptical of that all along. . . .

Deciding to let it slide, I cleared my throat. "Look, I haven't had a chance to talk to him yet," I said. "I need to figure out what to say first, and meanwhile he keeps barging up when I'm trying to, like, talk to Josh and stuff. So I was hoping you guys could help me out. You know—"

"Say no more." Chrissie held up one hand to stop me. "We're all over it. We'll do whatever it takes to distract him. Right, Cass?"

"Right," Cassie agreed promptly. "We'll make sure you have plenty of space to work on Josh. Just leave Ryan to us."

I actually felt a little better after my chat with the twins— like I had some allies, even if they didn't know the whole story. Unfortunately the feeling didn't last long. For one thing, I still had no idea what to do about Josh's raft plan. The more I thought about it, the more doubtful I was that anything good would come of it. In fact, when I tried to take a nap before dinner, I wound up having a way-too-vivid nightmare in which we all set out on a giant raft made of cardboard and tin cans. We wound up lost at sea, with no food or water, faced with all kinds of horrible stuff like whirlpools, rainstorms, tidal waves, and sharks. Well, actually the shark thing was the good part of the dream, since one of the people it chomped was Angela. But that was sort of beside the point.

I woke up to the sound of someone banging on the bottom of a pan—our island version of a dinner bell. Staggering to my feet, I left the shelter and headed for the fire pit, not feeling very rested at all.

By the time I made it there, Angela had already shoehorned herself into the seat beside Josh. Ned was sitting on his other side, which left me out in the cold. As usual.

With a sigh I sat down next to Mr. Truskey. He glanced over at me with a smile. "Good evening, Pauline," he said cheerfully. "How's the umbrella business today?"

I didn't even bother to try to figure that one out. "Just

Castaways

fine, Mr. T." I stared blankly at Macy, who was stirring something in a big metal pot. Ned and Kenny were helping her by setting out enough bowls, tin cans, and coconut shells to serve everyone. *So much for the work teams*, I noted rather gloomily. Macy was the only one from the current food-and-water team working on dinner. Cassie was nowhere to be seen, and as previously noted, Angela was way too busy flirting with Josh to pay any attention to the meal preparations.

Just then Ryan came loping toward the fire pit. He jumped over the empty log next to me and swept into what I guess was supposed to be a gallant bow. "Greetings, Dani," he said eagerly. "Is this seat free?"

I guess he took my blank stare to mean *Why yes, certainly, please sit down*, because he flopped down on the log. He immediately started babbling at me—I think it was something about the raft, though I wasn't sure. I was too busy trying to kick-start my still-sleepy brain so I could figure out what to do.

Then, salvation. The twins appeared, took in the situation with one glance, and swooped down on Ryan.

"Hi, Ry!" Cassie exclaimed with a giggle. To look at her, you would think she'd never been so happy to see someone in her life. "Can I sit here by you?"

She immediately squeezed herself onto the end of the log beside him. Meanwhile Chrissie pushed her way to his other side, bumping me down my own log in the process. "Hey, don't hog him, Cass!" she exclaimed with a pout. "I want to sit by Ryan too."

"It's okay." Ryan sounded kind of confused. "There's plenty of room for all of us."

"Oh, good." Cassie giggled again, tilting her head to one side as she gazed at Ryan adoringly. "I'm really glad."

"Yeah, me too, I guess." Ryan still seemed kind of perplexed by all the sudden attention, but he also looked as if he was maybe starting to enjoy himself a little. And no wonder. There were plenty of boys back at Tweedale Middle School who would've killed—or, at least, maimed—to have both Saunders twins fawning over them like that.

Meanwhile I just sat there, too tired to move or react or even think very much. All I could seem to do was stare across the fire at Josh and Angela and ponder the eternal question of how some girls seemed to be born knowing how to flirt. The twins were definitely among that group. And as much as I hated to admit it, so was Angela.

Castaways

I, on the other hand, was in Group B. B as in Baffled. Bewildered. And most of all, Bad at acting like a flirty little girly-girl. For a second I was tempted to Barge over there and Boot Angela in the Butt until she got away from my Boyfriend.

But I couldn't. Josh still hadn't given me the go-ahead to tell anyone about us, and that meant I had to just sit there, Bite my tongue, and watch as Angela giggled and slimed all over him. It was pretty depressing.

I sighed, almost wishing I could go back to the shark dream. So far, having a boyfriend wasn't really turning out to be much fun at all.

Seven

"Dani! Hey, Dani! Wait up!"

I winced. After sitting through an entire dinner watching Angela act like an adoring moon revolving around planet Josh, I was still feeling pretty low. Too low to be in the mood for dealing with Kenny.

However, I also didn't have the energy to try to escape, now that he'd followed me down the trail toward the stream. So I just stopped and waited for him to catch up.

"What?" I asked dully.

Kenny squinted at me suspiciously. "What's the matter with you?"

Castaways

"Nothing. Now, what do you want? I'm busy."

That wasn't exactly true. The only thing I was busy doing at the moment was removing myself from Angela's presence before I summoned up the energy to murder her.

"I still need to talk to you about my plan." Kenny's voice almost immediately ramped up to maximum whining velocity. "You keep leaving before I can finish."

I shrugged and sighed. I so wasn't in the mood for this.

Clearly taking my obvious depression to mean *Why yes, Kenny, please expound upon your lamebrain idea immediately,* he started babbling excitedly, repeating all the stuff he'd already told me about the boat and the other island.

"Yeah?" I interrupted after a moment. "So do you have anything to add? Because so far this isn't exactly breaking news, you know."

"Hold your horses. I was just getting to the new part." He frowned at me. "See, I thought of a *way* easier way to get rescued than building some stupid raft. We could build a giant fire up in that flat clearing where my zoo is. It's more than halfway to the top of the mountain, so if we make enough flames and smoke, they should be able to see it from that boat—"

"And on the other island too," I finished for him, sort

of intrigued in spite of myself. Surprised, too. It wasn't every day that Kenny came up with a decent plan that didn't involve humiliating me or getting out of chores.

"Yeah." Kenny looked pleased with himself. "That way we have twice as much chance of getting rescued. See?"

I hesitated, trying to come up with a flaw in Kenny's plan. But it actually made a lot of sense. A lot more sense than floating out to sea on some bloated, cobbled-together raft . . .

That thought jolted me back to reality. What was I doing? Kenny's idea might seem logical, but that was no reason to start running around like a chicken with my head cut off, changing plans willy-nilly. I might as well stick with Josh's raft for now—what did I have to lose, after all? If it worked, we'd be rescued and I wouldn't have to worry about it anymore. Even if it didn't work and we ended up trying the fire thing, at least I wouldn't have had to go against Josh. That seemed like win-win to me.

"Whatever," I muttered in my brother's general direction. "I still think you're making up this whole boat story anyway."

He rolled his eyes. "Don't be a ditz, Dani*elle*," he said. "Why would I make up something like that?"

Castaways

"Why do you do anything?" Not giving him much of a chance to ponder that philosophical gem, I turned away. "Anyway, I've got to go."

I hurried off into the jungle, not looking back until he was well out of sight among the trees.

The next day it was my work team's turn on food-and-water duty. That meant we had to get up early—with a little help from Ned's super-deluxe wristwatch alarm—to haul water from the stream, boil it so it would be safe to drink, and prepare something to eat for the whole group. Back home, cooking wasn't one of my top ten favorite activities. But since being on the island, I'd found that it was actually sort of fun. Well, not the getting-up-early part or the water hauling. But it was sort of cool to try to figure out new ways to serve the same old ingredients.

"What do you think?" Brooke peered at the bright green leaf Ned was holding.

Ned nibbled at the edges of the leaf, looking thoughtful. "I'm pretty sure this is the stuff," he said. "It tastes pretty good. Sort of spicy, almost."

"Cool!" I was doing my best not to think about Josh, Angela, Ryan, or Kenny. It wasn't easy, since together they made up more than a third of the population of the island. "Maybe we can cook the papaya in some water like the other group did yesterday, and season it with this stuff and some salt from the lagoon."

"Good idea." Brooke glanced at the pile of similar leaves on the food-prep table. "But we'll need a lot more of the greens than that. Is this all you picked, Ned?"

He shrugged, looking sheepish. "It seemed like more at the time."

"That's okay." I gave Ned a reassuring smile. "I'll run and get some more if you tell me where it is." Maybe Brooke was annoyed that Ned hadn't been aggressive enough with the hunting and gathering, but I was just impressed that he'd been able to identify the ordinary-looking leaves as edible. I'm no health-food nut or anything—when I order a vegetable in a restaurant, it's usually French fries. But after more than a week on the island most of us, myself most definitely included, were craving some variety in our diets.

Ned explained that the greens were growing in a little clearing just past the stream. I was heading toward the jungle, toting a large, empty duffel bag to use for carrying my haul, when I heard a soft voice calling my name.

Castaways

Turning my head, I saw Macy hurrying toward me. It was no surprise to see her up at that hour—she's totally one of those early-to-rise types. However, I was a little surprised when she said she wanted to talk to me. Macy and I had become better friends during our stay on the island, but that was sort of like saying that food gets better digested after you eat it. It's not that I disliked her before. To do that, she would've had to have been on my radar in the first place. Actually, though, getting to know her was one of the few positive things that had happened since crashing into that coral reef. Other than Josh, of course. And sometimes I wasn't even sure how positive that was.

Still, it wasn't as if Macy and I spent tons of time sharing heart-to-hearts about every detail of our lives. So I had no clue why she was looking all serious and begging for a few minutes of my time. "Okay," I said. "Can we walk while you talk?" I explained my errand.

Macy nodded and fell into step beside me as we entered the jungle, following the wide trail pounded flat in the underbrush by dozens of feet passing over it every day. She cleared her throat, shooting me a shy sidelong glance. "So Kenny came to talk to me last night . . . ," she began.

Isle Be Seeing You

I groaned. "Don't tell me. He wanted to tell you all about his brilliant fire plan, right?"

"It really does seem like a good idea." Macy's voice got even softer, almost disappearing into the continuous hum-buzz-drip of the jungle. "We could make a really big fire pile up there if we all worked together. Especially with all the wood that came down during the hurricane. It wouldn't take long at all."

I could almost hear the rest of her thought: *Not nearly as long as building the raft.*

"Hmm," I responded noncommittally. "Maybe."

She was silent for a moment, probably waiting for more. But I wasn't about to hand her Josh's pride and dignity on a silver platter. Even if I had a few doubts about the raft myself, I had more loyalty than that.

"Well," she went on at last, "I was just thinking about it, that's all. If you said something to Josh—"

"No way." This time I didn't hesitate before answering. "Josh is our leader, and he's totally into this raft plan. I think we should all support that."

"Oh." Macy sounded disappointed, but not particularly surprised. "Well, maybe you're right."

She paused for so long after that that I thought she'd

dropped it. In fact, my mind was wandering back to my own multitude of problems by the time she spoke again.

"But maybe we could do both."

"Huh?" I snapped back to the here and now. "Like I said, I'm not going to go against Josh on this. And I don't think anyone else should either. He's our leader, remember?"

"I know. And I'm not saying we have to oppose the raft plan or anything. But maybe the three of us—you, me, and Kenny, I mean—could, you know, work on the fire, too. Secretly. Just in case."

I tried to muster up some indignation at Macy's lack of faith in Josh. But I couldn't really pull it off. How could I blame her for doubting Josh's plan when I'd been doubting it like crazy myself since it first came out of his mouth?

Of course, that didn't mean I was going to let anyone know that. "No, thanks," I told Macy wearily, wishing that Ms. Watson would just hurry up and find us already so I wouldn't have to worry about either of the rescue plans. "You can waste your time believing in Kenny's little fantasy boat if you want. But leave me out of it, okay?"

Macy sighed softly. "All right. I just thought I'd ask."

Isle Be Seeing You

We located the greens, picked a whole bagful of them, and returned to camp in near silence. I thought that was going to be the end of that.

I was wrong.

Breakfast was another teeth-clencher of a meal. I was treated to the sight of Angela making goo-goo eyes at Josh almost nonstop. I did my best to distract myself from that repulsive sight by fantasizing about how great it would be when we finally got rescued and everything was out in the open. Would Angela freak out and cry when she heard about me and Josh, or get spitting mad, or maybe just spontaneously combust? I couldn't decide which of those options would be more satisfying—maybe she would do all three at once!

I was so busy with such deep thoughts that I wound up sitting around the fire pit longer than anyone else except Mr. Truskey, who had fallen asleep leaning back against one of the seating logs with his bowl of papaya porridge resting on his scrawny, sunburned chest. Finally becoming aware of the morning sun beating down on me, I got up, stepped carefully over the teacher's sprawled-out legs, and headed for the shade of the shelter.

Castaways

I stuck my head inside, absentmindedly wondering if it was too early for a nap. Seeing Mr. T snoozing peacefully away out there had given me ideas.

"Hi, Dani!" an eager voice greeted me.

I gulped. I'd almost forgotten about Ryan.

"Hi, Ryan," I said weakly. "Er, I have to go and—"

"Wait!"

Ryan leaped to his feet. Unfortunately he'd just been applying sunscreen to his legs, and the sudden movement sent the open bottle flying, splattering gooey white lotion everywhere. I jumped back just in time to avoid getting slimed.

"Oops, sorry," he said sheepishly, dabbing awkwardly at a creamy white blob on the shelter's rough wooden ceiling. "I just didn't want you to run off before I could talk to you. Did you have a chance to think about, you know, what I was saying the other day?"

My mouth opened and closed a few times; I'm sure I looked like some kind of clueless fish. My brain seemed to be working on about a fish level too. Staring into his eager face, I couldn't even imagine what I was supposed to say now. Somehow I figured "glub glub" wasn't going to cut it.

"Dani! Hey, sister-dork!"

I'd never been so glad to hear my little brother's voice in my life. "Oops! Excuse me," I told Ryan with what I hoped wasn't too obviously major big-time relief. "I'd better see what Kenny wants."

I ducked back out of the shelter. Kenny was standing there scratching his stomach, which was sticking out through a big hole in the front of his grubby T-shirt.

"Are you ever planning to change clothes during this whole trip?" I asked him. "There's a reason Mom and Dad packed you more than one outfit, you know."

He ignored the comment. "Listen, Dani," he said urgently. "Josh sent me to find you. He wants you to go meet him right now."

Panic twisted in my gut as I wondered if Kenny had somehow figured out about me and Josh and was mounting some horrible new prank. But he was gazing at me innocently.

"Really?" I said cautiously. "Er, what does he want?"

Kenny rolled his eyes. "How do I know what he wants? I'm not his stupid secretary."

"Fine, whatever." The panic was already subsiding. How would Kenny find out anything? Nobody knew except me and Josh. I certainly hadn't told my little brother any-thing, and we already know how Josh felt about spilling the secret. "So where is he?"

"Up at the ridge." Kenny shrugged. "Oh yeah, I guess maybe he wants to talk to you about the raft. Or some-thing. I think he's, like, looking for more wood, maybe."

Doing my best to hide my sudden attack of stomach but-terflies, I nodded. "Okay," I said, carefully keeping my voice casual. "Guess I'd better run up there and see what's up."

"Dani?" Ryan poked his head out of the shelter. "Are you—"

"Be right back!" I sang out, drowning out whatever he was going to say. Then I took off for the jungle, not slow-ing down until I was out of sight of the beach.

Then I slowed to a brisk walk, wondering what was going on now. Why was Josh summoning me up to the ridge? Was it just a way to get us some time alone? I wasn't sure why Josh would send a messenger—especially a notoriously unreliable one like Kenny—on that kind of errand.

Then again, if Josh was willing to trust Kenny with his message, maybe that meant he was coming around on the secrecy thing. My eyes widened as a new possibility

popped into my head. Maybe that was exactly what he wanted to talk about. Maybe he was ready to tell everyone about the two of us!

Crossing my fingers hopefully, I broke into a jog. Within minutes I was sweating in the dense humidity of the jungle. Why had Josh chosen such a distant spot for this meeting, anyway? I could have been to the butterfly spot three or four times already.

"Oh, well," I muttered under my breath. "At least maybe this means we won't have to worry about anyone else barging in on us, like Angela or—*Macy!*" I blurted out as I burst into the sunny clearing on the ridge and saw the other girl sitting on a large boulder. "What are you doing here?"

"Sorry, Dani," Macy said shyly. "I hate lying to anyone, especially someone nice like you. But we weren't sure how else to get you up here."

"We?" I repeated suspiciously.

Hearing the sound of running footsteps behind me, I glanced over my shoulder just in time to see Kenny burst out of the jungle. "Whoa!" he panted. "Living on this island is making you a lot less lazy, Dani. You got up here fast!"

I glared at him, then at Macy. "Okay, what's going on here?" I crossed my arms over my chest. "Where's Josh?"

Castaways

The two of them exchanged a glance. Macy looked worried, and Kenny looked smirky and amused. "Um, he's not here," Macy admitted. "We just needed a way to get you up here. Quickly. Sorry."

My face went red as I realized that Macy had used her inside knowledge about Operation Distract Josh against me—and worse yet, she'd apparently let Kenny in on it too. I wasn't sure whether to be furious at them for tricking me like that, or embarrassed that I'd fallen for their story hook, line, and sinker.

I was still trying to sort that out when Kenny let out a shout. "There it is!" he cried, pointing off toward the ocean.

Before I could figure out what he was talking about, Macy grabbed me firmly by the shoulders and spun me around so that I was facing in the same direction. "Look!" she commanded.

Before I could protest, a flash of sunlight sparkled off something out there in the water, making me squint. As I focused on the source of the sparkle, my jaw dropped.

"Whoa," I said blankly. "It's a boat!"

Eight

I just stared for a second, wonder-
ing if I was hallucinating. I'd heard that the tropical heat
could do that to you. But no—it was real. A large boat
was chugging along out in the open water beyond the
neighboring islands, its white sides and polished-chrome
accents standing out starkly against the sapphire blue
water. If I squinted hard, I could almost make out human
forms walking around on the broad deck. Okay, maybe
that was wishful thinking—it was too far away to make
out that much detail. But it seemed like a pretty safe bet
that those were people on board.

Castaways

"I can't believe it." I tore my gaze away from the boat to stare at my brother. "You were telling the truth about seeing a boat!"

He looked insulted. "Duh," he said sourly. "I only told you like a million times."

"Never mind," Macy said. "The important thing is, we're all on the same page now. So what are we going to do about it?"

She looked at me intently. I gulped, catching on to her meaning. I may be stubborn, but I'm not slow.

"I—I don't know." My mind raced along at a thousand miles an hour, storing, labeling, and categorizing this new information. All along I'd been assuming that even if Kenny wasn't making up the whole boat story, he was probably at least exaggerating whatever he'd seen. He tends to do that; my parents refer to it as his "creative spark," but I prefer to call it what it is—pathetic shouts for attention. In Kenny's nutty little mind, he could make a rescue boat out of a passing pelican or a white plastic bag floating along on the current. And Josh had been so busy directing the raft-building process that he hadn't had a chance to go up to the ridge himself and check it out yet, which meant we hadn't had any non-

Kenny-based proof that the boat existed at all.

Until now.

"Okay," I said slowly, still trying to digest this new development. "So there's a boat. That's cool. It means when Josh finishes the raft—"

"No!" Macy interrupted, looking alarmed. "Forget about the raft. What about the fire idea?"

"Well, I don't know. The raft plan is a better bet. Probably." The words sounded lame even as they left my lips.

Kenny wrinkled his nose. "Get real, *Danielle*," he said. "The raft will take forever to finish, and nobody even knows if it will float. The fire will be a lot easier."

"And safer." Macy gazed at me imploringly. "Just think about it, Dani, okay?"

I was already way ahead of her. For a few stubborn seconds I kept trying to convince myself that Josh's plan could work out just as well as Kenny's idea. But it was no use. All my potential arguments collapsed in the face of plain old common sense. Why risk our necks—and our tender, non-shark-chewed flesh—setting out on a rickety raft when there was an easier way? If we could build a fire big enough to be seen by either whoever was making the smoke on that other island or the people on the

boat, one or the other was sure to investigate. And before we knew it, we would be back home trying to forget we'd ever known what a choo-choo bug was.

"Okay. I see your point." Despite my rising excitement at the thought of imminent rescue, I felt like the world's biggest traitor as Josh's face flashed into my mind. Or should that be the world's worst girlfriend?

I pushed that out of my mind, deciding to look on the bright side: Once we were rescued, nobody would remember or care how it had come about.

"So are you with us?" Macy asked cautiously.

I nodded. "I'm in," I said. "But let's hurry, okay? We should try to get the fire going as soon as possible. Like way before the raft is ready to go."

Macy looked worried. "I'm not sure we can do that." She glanced around the ridge, which was rocky and exposed, a large bare spot in the sea of vegetation that covered most of the island. "There's not much wood up here, which means we'll have to carry it all up from the jungle. If we want the fire to be big enough for anyone to see, that means a lot of wood. And with only three of us working on it . . ."

She didn't finish, but that was okay. Nobody needed to

draw me a picture to make my options clear. I could sneak around behind Josh's back, hope we could pull it off in time and that he wouldn't be mad at me when he figured it out. Or I could do the right thing and talk to him.

He's a sensible guy, I told myself. *He'll see that this is the best way to go. Won't he?*

I took a deep breath. "Okay. I'll go talk to Josh right now."

Macy smiled. "Great," she said, sounding relieved. "Thanks, Dani. We'll get to work up here until you report back. Right, Ken?"

I left them gathering sticks at the edge of the ridge. Even though the trip back to the beach was all downhill, I moved a lot slower than I had going up. I was looking forward to this conversation about as much as a pig looks forward to becoming pork chops. Maybe less.

Deciding to practice a little, I cleared my throat. "Listen, Josh," I said to a passing choo-choo bug. "I don't want to hurt your feelings or anything, but your raft idea stinks. My eight-year-old twerp of a brother came up with a much better plan. . . . Wait." Taking a deep breath, I started again, this time addressing the lizard that was scurrying frantically down the path ahead of me. "Okay, Josh, I need to be honest with you. You know that raft

you're building? You'll be lucky if it makes it as far as the coral reef. So here's an idea that might actually work...."

I shook my head. Maybe it was better not to practice.

When I reached the beach most of the others were gathered at Raft Central. Josh was helping Ryan tie pieces of wood together, while Ned and the twins busily duct-taped the life jackets. Angela, of course, was standing around being useless.

None of them had noticed me approaching yet. I watched them work, trying to psyche myself up for what I had to do. How hard could it be? All I had to do was tell them what I'd just seen up on the ridge, then convince them to ditch the raft thing and help build the fire.

Taking a deep breath, I hurried forward. Josh was the first to spot me. He looked up at me and smiled.

"Hi, Dani!" he said, sounding really happy to see me. "Where've you been? We were all just wondering."

"I—I—," I stammered lamely. I'd been all ready to blurt out what was on my mind. But that first look at Josh's open, happy face stopped me in my tracks. If I said what I needed to say in front of all those other people, it would embarrass him half to death. I couldn't do that to him.

Angela wrinkled her nose at me. "Yeah, we were won-

dering if you were planning to do any work today at all."

I glared at her. She was the last one who should be complaining about other people being lazy. But I didn't have time to point that out to her. Instead I turned back to Josh.

"Listen," I told him, trying to sound casual. "I just found a new spot with a big bunch of wood out in the jungle. It looks like it might work for the raft. Want to come see?"

Ryan immediately jumped forward. "I can go with her and check it out if you want, Josh," he volunteered eagerly.

I gulped. "Er . . . ," I began.

"No!" Cassie blurted out. As everyone glanced at her in surprise, she smiled sheepishly. "I mean, don't go, Ryan. Stay here with us."

"Yeah, it's okay, Ry," Josh added calmly. "I'd better go look myself. You can keep working on the rudder, okay?"

Ryan looked a little disappointed, but he shrugged. "Sure."

I saw the twins exchange a relieved glance. Angela didn't look quite so pleased, but she didn't say anything as Josh and I headed up the beach toward the jungle.

We stepped into the shade of the trees side by side and made our way down the trail. Within a few minutes

we were well out of sight and sound of the beach. That was when Josh reached over and took my hand in his as we walked.

He glanced over at me, suddenly looking a little shy. "So is there really a pile of wood out here?" he asked.

"No." Taking a deep breath, I tried to figure out how to proceed. I decided maybe it was like ripping off a Band-Aid—better to do it quickly. "Listen, Josh, I have to talk to you. It's important."

He stopped and turned to face me, grabbing my other hand as well. "I want to talk to you about something too." His deep brown eyes suddenly looked all sincere, and his voice sounded a little choked up as he continued. "When we got stranded on this island, I thought it was the worst thing ever, you know? But now I'm glad it happened. Otherwise I might never have figured out how cool you are, or had the guts to tell you. You know?"

"Wow." I wasn't sure what to say to that. Talk about being thrown off track. "I—well, yeah. Me too."

He smiled. "It's also totally cool how we're working on this raft together. I mean, I know everybody else is helping too, but I'm sort of thinking about it as our project, you know? You've been, like, so supportive and helpful

and stuff, and it's really cool. In fact"—he paused, look-ing shy again—"I wasn't going to tell you yet, but . . . well, I already decided I want to dedicate the raft to you when it's finished. People always give girls' names to boats and stuff, so I thought we could call it, like, Dani's Dream or something like that." He shot me an apologetic look. "Oh, but I haven't told the others that, of course. It'll be, like, our secret."

"Of course," I murmured, totally confused by now. Somehow, what I'd meant to be a serious talk about switching over to the fire idea had turned into a rah-rah session for the raft. And for me.

While I was still puzzling over that one, Josh took a step closer, his hands tightening on mine. I blinked at him stupidly, not sure for a moment what he was doing.

Then he leaned forward, his eyes drooping half closed. My heart raced as his face loomed closer and closer. I finally snapped my own eyes shut as his lips touched mine, feeling surprisingly soft and warm. . . .

And this time there was no Angela around to interrupt.

I guess most girls probably spend a lot of time imagin-ing what their first kiss will be like. For instance, my best friend Tina always says she wants hers to take place in a

pretty flower garden under the moonlight. And even though she already kissed this one guy on a dare last year, my other best friend, Michelle, thinks it would be cool to have her first *real* kiss on a train platform. Don't ask me what that's about, but hey, it's her fantasy, not mine.

As for me, well, I'd never really put a lot of thought into it. But now that it was happening, I knew that I couldn't have imagined anything more perfect than the reality. I mean, what could be better than standing in a sun-dappled little clearing in a tropical jungle while the coolest guy in the world gives you your first kiss? Okay, so maybe I wouldn't have chosen the sweat dripping down my back or the large choo-choo bug buzzing around our heads. But the rest was pretty amazing. Oh, and not that I had any basis for comparison, but Josh was an awfully good kisser.

Finally we pulled apart, both of us a little red faced and bashful, but happy. "That was nice," Josh whispered.

I nodded, still a little stunned about what had just happened. Happy stunned, of course. "Uh-huh."

"Oh!" Josh blinked. "Sorry, I forgot you wanted to talk to me about something too. What was it?"

I gulped, reality crashing down on me once again. After

what had just happened, there was no way I could say what I'd meant to say. No way I could risk ruining this moment. No. Way.

"Erp," I blurted out. "Uh, I mean, it's nothing. That is, I just wanted to tell you the same sort of thing. You know."

"Oh, okay." Josh smiled at me. "Cool."

Luckily he didn't seem suspicious at all, as he leaned in for another kiss.

Nine

I guess maybe all the kissing must have immobilized part of my brain, because I managed to completely forget about reporting back to Macy and Kenny. It wasn't until I saw their faces, wearing matching anxious expressions, that I remembered. Actually, only Macy's face looked anxious. Kenny looked more annoyed, and maybe a little constipated. Then again, he often looks like that.

"Hey, Dani. There you are!" Macy called, hurrying toward me with Kenny on her heels. I was standing at the fire pit carefully pouring a bucket full of water into our metal water-boiling pot to start lunch. Brooke and Ned were over at the food-prep area debating whether to boil or roast today's coconut course.

I looked up at Macy with a guilty smile. The lost part of my brain kicked back into gear instantly, and I realized it had been more than two hours since I'd left them up at the ridge. "Oh," I said lamely. "Er, there you are. I was looking for you before."

That was a bald-faced lie, but Macy seemed willing to let it slide. Kenny, however, was another story.

"Where did you look?" he demanded, his hands on his hips. "We've been up at the ridge all morning!"

"Shh!" Macy cast a worried look toward Brooke and Ned. "Never mind that. Did you talk to him, Dani?"

"Not exactly." I pretended to be very busy pouring so I wouldn't have to look her in the eyes. "Er, I sort of changed my mind about that."

"What are you talking about?" Kenny exclaimed.

Brooke glanced up curiously. But I guess she figured the commotion was just me and Kenny arguing as usual, because she shrugged and turned back to Ned almost immediately.

"Quiet, Kenny, please," Macy murmured. "Maybe we

should all go somewhere more private and talk about this a little."

I shrugged, carefully kicking the pot of water a little farther into the fire. "There's really nothing to talk about," I muttered. Not anything I felt like discussing with the two of them, anyway. I wasn't about to admit to them that I was wussing out because I didn't want to risk messing things up with Josh. I could barely admit that even to myself.

"But, Dani . . . ," Macy began uncertainly.

"Don't be a dork, Danielle," Kenny added.

I rolled my eyes. "Look, I just decided it was better to do both things. Two plans have got to be better than one, right? It means twice the chance of success."

Macy looked dubious about that one. "Well, maybe. But we still should tell Josh that we—"

"Look, I'll still help you guys with the fire and everything," I interrupted, noticing the others approaching from the direction of Raft Central. Josh was leading the way, with Angela hovering right around his left shoulder like a hungry choo-choo bug. "But only on one condition. We have to keep it a secret from everybody else. Especially Josh."

Isle Be Seeing You

Macy blinked and opened her mouth. Then she shut it again. Then she said, "Huh?"

"Take it or leave it," I said firmly, crossing my arms over my chest. "The fire plan stays a secret, or you two are on your own." I figured that was the only way to go. Then I could work on both plans, and Angela wouldn't be able to turn it against me.

Kenny glared at me and opened his mouth, ready to argue some more. But Macy had spotted the others coming our way too, and she grabbed him by the arm and shushed him.

"Do we have a deal?" I asked her.

She nodded, looking a little confused. I turned away to check on the water, but the next time I glanced back at her, she and Kenny were whispering together urgently.

I shrugged. Let them whisper. What did I care, as long as they kept their mouths shut? The only one whose opinion mattered to me was Josh, and as far as he knew, I was still totally on his team.

"Lift!" Brooke cried urgently. "Come on, Dani. Put some muscle into it, girl, What's wrong with you?"

"Sorry," I panted, doing my best to hoist the end of the

log I was holding a little higher. It wasn't easy. I'd just spent two hours in the midday sun hauling firewood up to the ridge, and my muscles felt like Silly Putty. Of course, everybody at Raft Central thought I'd been taking a nap that whole time, so they weren't too sympathetic to my plight.

Angela watched critically as Ryan and I moved the log into place. "Careful, Dani," she snapped. "If you drop that thing, you'll wreck the part beneath it."

"Gee, thanks for the advice." I was so busy trying not to drop the log on the raft—or my own foot—that the words didn't come out quite as sarcastically as I'd intended. But Angela shot me a sour look anyway.

Josh stepped forward to help as the log settled into place. "Great job, guys," he said with a special, though all too brief, smile just for me.

"Okay, let's get the next one." Ryan was already reaching for an even bigger log. I swear, that boy never runs out of energy. He could probably finish the raft on his own, swim back to the mainland, run a marathon, and still be ready to jump up and dance a jig. Not that I know what a jig is, exactly, but it sounds sort of energetic, just like Ryan.

"Give me a minute," I mumbled, rubbing my aching

arms. If I kept going at this rate, I was going to have muscles like Arnold Schwarzenegger by the time I got back to civilization.

Josh glanced at me with concern. "Are you okay?" he asked. "Maybe we should switch off—let someone else lift for a while."

"Good idea. Maybe Ned could—" Brooke broke off, glancing around. "Hey, where'd Ned go, anyway?" she grumbled. "He said he'd be right down to help, after he finished cleaning up from lunch."

Angela snorted. "He probably stuck all the dishes in the stream, then settled down to take a nap while the current rinses them off," she said. "I mean, I hate to come right out and call anyone lazy, but . . ." She pursed her lips into a prissy little O.

I winced on Ned's behalf. I happened to know that he was up at the ridge at that moment. Macy and Kenny had asked if we could let him and only him in on the fire plan, and I'd okayed it. Ned wasn't the type to go around blabbing to people, and besides, he was really turning out to be a huge help—not only in collecting firewood, but in actually arranging it into something that might burn successfully.

"For your information, I just saw Ned," I spoke up. "He's busy hauling water from the stream. Figured he'd get a jump on dinner."

"Really?" Brooke looked surprised. "That's weird. I thought we had plenty of water."

Oops. "Um, Kenny tripped over the big pot and spilled it all over," I clarified quickly. "So he's helping Ned get more."

"Oh. Well, I guess that's all right, then." Brooke seemed mollified. The others were obviously less than enthralled with my fascinating rendition of Ned Gets Water, Part 2.

I let out a silent sigh of relief as everyone started discussing the best way to move the rest of the larger logs into place. I was getting pretty good at coming up with cover stories lately; I only hoped I could keep it up for another day or so. That would give us enough time to get the burn pile ready to go. Then it would only be a matter of time before we were all back home enjoying electricity, flush toilets, non-papaya-based food, and all the other privileges of civilization. And in my case, watching Angela fume every time she saw me and Josh together.

The thought gave me strength. Well, mental strength,

anyway. I sighed, willing my tired arm muscles to keep functioning as we got back to work.

A couple of hours later the twins found me as I was rinsing my sweaty, bright red face in the stream. "Hey," Chrissie greeted me with a little frown. "What are you doing hiding out back here?"

"Trying not to die of heat stroke," I retorted, dunking both wrists underwater. Ned claimed that was supposed to help somehow, and I wasn't about to question him. He'd read more useful facts on the Internet than most of us could find in the school library. Most of them even seemed to be true. "Why do you ask?"

Cassie's eyes were wide and worried. "Angela's hanging all over Josh out on the beach."

"So what else is new?" I muttered, swiping one wet arm across my forehead.

The twins sighed and exchanged one of their patented twinny we-understand-all-you-understand-nothing glances. It's one of their more annoying habits, actually.

"Yes, that's pretty much our point," Chrissie told me with exaggerated patience. "The more time Angela

spends swooning all over him and telling him how great he is, the more likely she is to get him before he ever notices you."

Gritting my teeth, I once again resisted the urge to let them know that he'd almost certainly noticed me while the two of us were liplocked out in the jungle. Swallowing my words that way was starting to give me big-time indigestion.

But even more stomach-churning was the thought that they might be right. How would I even know if Josh's feelings were changing? I hadn't been anywhere near alone with him since that little kissing session a couple of days earlier, thanks to the Secret Pact. And despite my best efforts to keep them apart, Angela couldn't possibly spend more time at Josh's side if she'd stapled herself to him. What if her near-constant presence wore him down, as the twins feared? Could her evil powers possibly overwhelm his good taste?

The thought made me feel crankier than ever. "Look, get off my case, okay?" I snapped at the twins. "I can't control what stupid Angela does. Or Josh either."

The twins looked wounded. "Fine, whatever," Chrissie said.

Isle Be Seeing You

"Yeah," Cassie added. "We're just trying to help."

"Sorry," I muttered, even though I was still feeling irritated. Not so much at them—Cassie was right, they were only trying to help—but at myself. What was happening to me, anyway? I hated feeling so girly-girl and pathetic, worrying so much about what Josh thought of me or what Angela might do that I was practically paralyzed with anxiety. Keeping my true thoughts and feelings to myself instead of sharing them with whoever would listen. The real me wouldn't act that way.

So why couldn't I seem to snap out of it?

By just before dinnertime the next day, I was feeling much more optimistic. "You think it's big enough?" I asked, gazing at the tremendous pile of tree branches, driftwood, dry leaves, palm fronds, and assorted other combustibles that now took up at least half of the rocky bare expanse of the ridge.

"I think it's ready." Macy's eyes were shining with quiet excitement.

"Me too," Kenny added.

Ned nodded. "Yep."

It was a rare moment when all four of us were up there

together. The others were cooking, resting, or washing up before dinner and none of us were on food duty that day, which meant no one would miss us for a while. We'd taken advantage of that to whip ourselves into a frenzy of kindling collecting and branch arranging.

Ned nodded. "We could try lighting it tomorrow morning right after breakfast. That way it should be going strong by the time the boat goes by."

"Excellent," I murmured. Suddenly rescue was so close I could almost taste it. We would light the fire tomorrow, someone would see it, and before we knew it, we'd be home again. Seeing our families. Sleeping on actual beds. Mr. Truskey could get the choo-choo germs flushed out of him and go back to his usual state of near sanity. And of course, the extra-special bonus—as soon as we were back in the real world, Josh and I could go public, I could enjoy the resulting Angela meltdown, and everything would be back to normal. I could hardly wait.

When we returned to the beach, we found the others sitting around the fire pit talking about the raft. "And we still need to figure out how to attach the rudder. Once that's worked out, I'm hoping to have it finished with

another good day's work," Josh was saying eagerly. "Maybe two days at the most."

My fellow fire builders and I exchanged a quick glance when the others weren't looking. Talk about cutting it close . . .

But it didn't matter. As long as we could get the fire lit in time for the boat to see it on its next daily pass, our plan would still work out just fine.

"Awesome, Josh!" Angela leaned closer and squeezed his arm. "That's all thanks to you. This raft is going to be so amazing."

I closed my eyes so I wouldn't have to watch her make eyelash-fluttering goo-goo eyes at him any longer. As far as I was concerned, the rescuers couldn't possibly come soon enough.

"Almost ready?" Macy whispered as she passed me on her way out of the shelter early the next morning.

I was sitting there, bleary-eyed, staring at the laces on my sneakers because it just seemed like too much effort to tie them. Every muscle in my body ached like crazy. Even my face muscles felt sore when I yawned. I'd

thought I was in pretty good shape—back home I worked out with the rest of the basketball team almost every day. But basketball muscles were no match for the work I'd done over the past few days, running back and forth trying to do my share on two huge, difficult projects. Three, actually, if you counted trying to keep Angela from glomming onto Josh 24-7 like some kind of big, blond parasite.

But it would all be worth it, I reminded myself. Today was the day.

I reached forward and tied my shoes, groaning softly as my back and arm muscles creaked. Straightening up again, I glanced around the shelter. The twins were sound asleep nearby, curled up together like kittens. A few feet away Mr. T was lying on his back, his mouth hanging open, snoring loudly. Ned, Macy, and Kenny had already tiptoed out.

Josh, Ryan, and Brooke were already up and gone too, which was no surprise. Brooke was almost always the first one awake. And the two boys often went for a jog together before breakfast. However, my eyes narrowed as I noticed that Angela was missing as well. Unlike the other three, she wasn't exactly known as an early riser.

Isle Be Seeing You

Then again, neither was I. Stifling another yawn, I flicked myself in the cheeks a few times with my fingers, trying to wake myself up. After dinner the night before, the four of us in the fire-building faction had huddled briefly to finalize our plans. We'd agreed to get up early and sneak up to the ridge to check on our fire pile and take care of any finishing touches. That way the fire would be ready to go right after breakfast. I shivered, and only partly because of the cool early-morning sea breeze.

I crawled out of the shelter and caught up with Macy just outside. The sun was rising above the horizon but hadn't yet had time to burn off all the night air, making the beach feel sort of misty-cool and pleasant. Brooke was over at the fire pit stoking up the embers, and Kenny and Ryan were down by the water untangling one of the fishing lines. All of them were well out of earshot.

"Listen," I told Macy, keeping my voice low just in case. "I've been thinking. When you all explain about the fire and stuff, I'm going to pretend I didn't know anything about it, okay?"

She looked surprised. "What? What do you mean, Dani? I thought we all agreed to tell the truth about it as soon as the others notice the smoke."

"You guys *can* tell the truth." I knew Macy took truth telling seriously. She's one of the most honest people I've ever met. "I'll just keep quiet about my part."

That was a conclusion I'd reached the night before, after lying awake worrying about our plans. My gaze drifted to the mountain rising in the center of the island. If Ned's calculations were right, our giant fire would quickly begin to emit huge clouds of smoke that would be visible for miles around. We'd sort of figured that just seeing that would be enough to convince the raft builders that rescue would be on the way before long. And to help explain why we'd done it.

But would it really explain *everything*? The more I thought about it, the more I realized that the answer to that question was no. Not even close. What would the others think when they realized that we'd all been keeping our plan a secret from them?

What would Josh think?

I bit my lip. Had it been a huge mistake to keep the fire plan a secret? When I'd made the others agree to that, I'd mostly been thinking of avoiding Angela's obnoxious comments. But now, the closer we got to putting our plan into action, the more clearly I could imagine the

awkward moment when Josh figured out what was going on. Had I betrayed him? I didn't really think so. But I wasn't sure he would agree, and I couldn't take any chances. Maybe when we got back home, I would figure out a way to tell him, but until then, it just seemed easier to play dumb.

Macy was still staring at me worriedly. "But Dani . . . ," she began.

"What are you guys talking about?"

Luckily it was Ned. Macy told him what I'd just told her.

"Oh." Ned looked confused. "But why don't you want them to know, Dani? You should get credit for all the hard work you did."

"It's okay," I insisted. "Really. My mind is totally made up, okay? I'm going to talk to Kenny about it too."

Macy sighed. "Okay, Dani. If that's really what you want."

"Yeah," Ned added.

I could tell they still didn't understand. But that was okay. Later on I could probably figure out a way to explain it to them.

Luckily none of the other early risers were paying much attention to us, and we managed to slip away from the beach without arousing suspicion. We gathered at

the ridge, but there wasn't much to do other than tuck in some dry leaves that had blown around a little during the night.

"Okay, then." Macy glanced around our little group. "We'll meet up here again after breakfast, right?"

"Except for me," I reminded them.

Ned shrugged. "Except for you."

When we got back to the beach, we found the fire pit almost deserted. I wandered into the shelter—which was empty—to change into my bathing suit. I was planning to be going for an innocent swim in the lagoon when my coconspirators made their big announcement.

I returned to the fire pit. "Where is everyone?" I asked the twins, who were perched on a log, eating bowls of papaya-colored mush.

Chrissie stirred her food and yawned. "Ryan finished eating already and went down to fish," she mumbled sleepily. "Mr. Truskey's still sleeping, I think. Dunno about anyone else."

"Brooke's over there," Cassie added helpfully, pointing toward the food-prep table, where Brooke was prying open a coconut. "Oh, and there's Ned coming now."

I grabbed a bowl and helped myself to some mush. Don't

get me wrong; I noticed right away that the only two people missing were Josh and Angela. But I didn't worry about it too much at that moment. I figured she was just up to her usual shenanigans, keeping him company while he washed his face in the stream or something. It was annoying, but I comforted myself with the fact that it would be over soon. Besides, my grumbling stomach seemed like a much more urgent issue at the moment.

Ned, Macy, and Kenny joined the twins and me at the fire pit. Brooke wandered back over eventually too. We were all still eating when we heard a triumphant cry from farther down the beach.

"Whazzat?" Cassie asked through yet another yawn. "Did Ry catch another baby shark or something?"

But it wasn't Ryan who was racing toward us. It was Angela. Josh was right behind her, and both of them had huge grins on their faces.

"Big news, guys!" Angela cried breathlessly as she reached us. "Like, huge!"

"What?" I muttered. "Did you figure out how to turn coconut juice into nail polish or something?"

She ignored me. By this time Josh had arrived too, and she grabbed his arm and dragged him forward. "Check it

Castaways

out," Angela exclaimed giddily. "You know how Josh figured we wouldn't be able to finish the raft until, like, this afternoon or even later?"

"Uh-huh," a few people responded.

"Well, guess what?" Angela grinned proudly. "Josh and I worked like crazy last night and got up extra early this morning to finish it as a surprise for everyone!"

There were gasps and exclamations all around as that sunk in. I just sat there silently, stunned at the news. For a moment all I could focus on was the "Josh and I" part. Why hadn't I noticed any of this going on right under my nose? So much for keeping her away from him . . .

Then Josh stepped forward, looking excited. "That's right," he said. "The raft is ready to go, the weather's perfect, so we shouldn't waste any time. I'm thinking we should go ahead and launch it right now! Who's with me?"

Ten

For a moment I was too shocked to respond. You know how people say "my mind was a blank?" Well, now I know what that means. It was like the Sahara Desert had suddenly unrolled in my brain, covering over every thought that had ever been there. Or maybe it was more like my mind had turned into a giant chalkboard with nothing written on it. Or a vast ocean, deep blue and endless. You get the picture.

I finally noticed that Josh was looking at me, smiling eagerly. My brain creaked back into gear, and I realized he was expecting me to volunteer to accompany him on the raft's maiden—and perhaps only—voyage.

"I'll do it!"

It actually took me several seconds to realize that I wasn't the one who'd spoken. After all, I'd meant to. I really, really had. My mouth was even hanging open, all ready to say the words.

But someone else had beaten me to it.

"I'll do it," Angela said again, a simpering smile on her face. "I'll go with you, Josh. I'm not scared—as long as you're going with me."

That jolted me out of my daze. I leaped forward a few steps, stubbing my toe on one of the seating logs and almost buying myself a quick trip to Dirtsville. Or, rather, Sandsville. "No, me!" I blurted out, lurching toward Josh. "I'll go!"

Ryan had heard the commotion by now and wandered over to see what was happening. He caught on quickly. "Me too!" he cried, looking as thrilled as if Josh was asking for someone to accompany him to the Happy Land of Free Ice Cream and DVDs.

A couple of the others volunteered at that point as well, but unlike Ryan and Angela, they didn't sound very enthusiastic about the idea. I couldn't really blame them;

it wasn't as if I was looking forward to it either. Especially the sharks.

Angela was glaring around at everyone except Josh. "I already said I'd go, people," she snitted. "I mean, come on. You've all seen the raft. It's not like all of us will fit."

I was already irritated enough at her attitude. But whenever she used that particular I'm-way-too-perfect-for-the-rest-of-you tone, I just saw red. And this time was no exception. "Oh, yeah?" I put my hands on my hips and glared right back at her. "Well, this isn't Princess Angela's world, you know. Just because you said you'd go, doesn't mean—"

"Hey!" Josh interrupted, sounding anxious. "Maybe we should go check out the raft and talk about it down there, okay?"

It was pretty obvious that he was trying to head off World War Three erupting right there on the beach. But it worked. Just hearing his voice reminded me that I needed to keep control of my temper. I wasn't about to let Evil Angela drag me down to her level and make me look stupid in front of everyone.

"Sure," I said as calmly as I could manage. "Let's go."

"Fine," Angela added through tight, pursed little lips.

Most of the others looked relieved. Well, except for Kenny—he looked a little disappointed. Kind of the same way he always looked when Mom and Dad refused to let him watch professional wrestling on TV.

"Whoo-hoo!" Ryan crowed, leaping forward to lead the way. "Superraft, here we come!"

We all trooped down the beach to Raft Central. As I walked, I found myself hoping that Josh and Angela really had worked a miracle overnight. Maybe they'd fixed up the raft so much that I would change my mind about the whole plan.

But as soon as I saw it, my heart sank. The raft consisted mostly of large tree branches lashed together with rope, twine, vines from the jungle, and even somebody's kneesocks. The life jackets from the boat made odd-looking pontoons lashed to each corner. Josh had even created a rudder out of a large, thin, flat piece of slate, which appeared to be attached to the rest of the craft with a single piece of string. The raft really wasn't bad considering what we'd had to work with on the island. But it still looked like something a bunch of hyperactive kindergarteners might throw together during recess. I couldn't imagine it floating at all, let alone making it across a mile or two of open sea.

Sneaking a peek at the others, I saw my own doubt reflected on several faces. However, some others just looked excited.

"Looks great, Josh!" Ryan was definitely part of the latter group. "The rudder is awesome!"

"Um, yeah." I swallowed hard, figuring I might as well get it over with. "So, come on, Josh—I'm ready to go."

"What are you talking about?" Angela demanded instantly. "You're not going. I am."

I turned to face her. "Forget it, Barnes. I'm the one who's going, and that's that."

Angela glared back at me. "You?" she said. "Why should you be the one to go? I'm the one who worked the hardest on this raft. Well, other than Josh, of course." She glanced over at Josh with a sickly sweet smile.

"Oh, yeah? For your information, I did plenty of work while you were busy plucking your chin hairs or whatever it is you do down by the stream for three hours every morning," I retorted hotly.

"Whatever, Dani." Her voice practically dripped with disdain. "Do us all a favor and try real hard to grow up now, okay?"

Castaways

She rolled her eyes and smirked, obviously pleased with her own stupid retort. Suddenly, just like that, every rotten, snotty, downright evil thing she'd ever done flashed into my mind all at once, almost overwhelming me. "Shut up!" I cried. "You're just jealous because it's totally obvious that I should go, since I'm the one—"

Out of the corner of my eye, I saw Josh blanch as he realized what I was about to say. I cut myself off just in time with an audible gulp. What was wrong with me? I was letting Angela get to me. I'd almost blurted out the truth about me and Josh, just like that, in front of everyone.

Taking advantage of my momentary confusion, Josh stepped forward and spoke up quickly. "Listen, I just had a great idea," he said. "Why don't all three of us go? After all, the three of us are coleaders, right? It totally makes sense."

Some of my irritation at Angela shifted briefly in Josh's direction. Why couldn't he just get over the whole secrecy thing already?

But he was smiling so sincerely that my anger faded quickly. "Besides, we made two oars, remember?" he added. "With three of us aboard, two of us can paddle and the other person can steer. That should make things easier."

He had a point there. I just wished the third person

could be somebody else. A leper. An ax murderer. Even my math teacher. Pretty much anybody but Evil Angela.

"Okay," I said reluctantly. "I guess that makes sense. Sort of."

Angela didn't look completely thrilled at the idea of sharing a smallish raft with me, either, but she nodded. "Whatever you say, Josh."

Just then I noticed Kenny watching me, his forehead crinkled into a little V-wrinkle of anxiety. I bit my lip, belatedly remembering our fire plan. I glanced over at Macy and Ned. Macy was staring downward, seemingly fascinated by the sight of her own feet. Ned's mouth was hanging open slightly as he stared at me uncertainly.

I quickly shifted my gaze away from the three of them, and turned slightly so I couldn't see them even out of the corner of my eye. For a few moments there I'd totally forgotten about that fire pile up on the ridge. Oops. Of course I felt pretty guilty about it. But what could I do? For a second I dared to hope that one of them might speak up. If they told the others about the fire idea right now, convinced them how well it could work . . .

But no. Looking at that trio, I knew it wasn't going to happen. Macy was way too shy to speak up like that. Ned

was too passive. And Kenny? Even if he did say something, I doubted the others would listen to him in their current state of excitement over the raft. I guess Kenny must have realized that too, because he didn't say a word.

Shoving aside the feeling that I was betraying them, I smiled grimly at Josh. "Okay. So let's go already before we miss that boat."

While Chrissie went running back to the supply cave for the paddles Ryan had carved out of a couple of appropriately shaped tree branches, the rest of us pushed the raft down the slight slope of the beach toward the water's edge. I held my breath as the first tiny waves lapped over it, then as it scraped over the wet sand into the slightly deeper water. We gave it one last shove, and it swooshed away from the ground and floated, bobbing up and down in the gentle surf.

"Yay!" Cassie clapped her hands and giggled. "It works!"

Angela snorted, but Josh smiled. He splashed out a little farther, grabbing the side of the raft to steady it. "Climb aboard, ladies," he called, giving a little half bow.

"Why, thank you, kind gentleman," Angela simpered, sloshing forward.

"Give me a break," I muttered under my breath. Wading

out to the raft, I swung myself aboard. The raft shuddered a little under my weight, but it stayed afloat.

Ryan churned his way out through the surf, holding both the handmade paddles. "You sure you don't need another person?" he asked rather wistfully.

"Sorry, dude." Josh slapped him on the shoulder. "I'm not sure she'll hold any more. Anyway, the people here will need you to catch fish for them—even if we make it to the boat or the other island, it might still be a day or so before the rescuers can get here."

"Oh, yeah." Ryan looked pleased at the thought. "I can do that."

I smiled at Josh as he swung aboard, relieved by how he'd handled Ryan just then. The last thing I wanted to do was deal with *that* whole situation while trapped on a raft in the middle of the ocean with Angela and Josh as my audience.

I also found myself thinking about what a cool guy Josh really was. He truly cared about other people's feelings. No matter what, he always tried to make everyone feel good, from Ryan to Brooke to Kenny. How could I quibble if he seemed to care even about the feelings of an evil being from another dimension like Angela?

Castaways

Then I glanced out to sea and started to feel nervous again. Did I really believe we could ride that rickety raft all the way over to the other island, let alone out to the passing boat? If I thought about that question too hard, it started to give me the screaming heebie-jeebies. So I tried not to think about it anymore. Instead I grabbed one of the paddles Ryan was holding out to us and gripped it tightly. At least if we sank, maybe I could use the paddle to fight off the sharks.

"Okay, here goes," Josh said, interrupting my morbid thoughts. He draped one leg off the back of the raft and shoved off the shallow lagoon floor, sending us drifting out away from the beach.

"Bon voyage, you guys!" Cassie cried, waving at us vigorously as she stood ankle-deep in the surf.

"Be careful!" Brooke added.

At first things went surprisingly well. Josh took control of the rudder, which actually seemed to work the way it was supposed to. I wielded my paddle, digging into the crystal clear water and sending fish and crustaceans fleeing before me. The paddling was slow going, but for once Angela was actually doing her fair share of the work—probably because Josh was right there watching—and

between the two of us, we managed to work up to some decent forward momentum.

As we zoomed toward the coral reef that encircled the lagoon, the faint sound of cheering drifted over the water from the direction of the beach. I glanced back between strokes and saw most of our fellow castaways jumping up and down and waving their arms happily. I smiled, feeling a little more optimistic myself all of a sudden. We were doing it! Okay, so we weren't even all the way across the lagoon yet, but still, we were doing it. The raft was still afloat, the rudder was working, we were on our way. Maybe, just maybe, all my teeth gnashing and angst had been for nothing.

"Check it out, you guys," Josh said excitedly. "We're almost to the reef already. I think this is going to work!"

I almost reached down and knocked on the rough wooden floor of the raft. I knew a jinx when I heard one, and I was afraid he'd just jinxed us big-time. But I didn't want to lose my paddling rhythm, so I didn't knock on wood after all.

Big mistake.

We were only a few yards from the reef, but I hardly saw the craggy shapes of the coral sticking out of the

water. Instead I stared out past the reef, hypnotized by the rougher waves of the deep water beyond. Were they always that big? From the beach, the ocean looked as smooth as the average bathtub. But up close it was a different story.

"Pay attention, Dani," Angela snapped at me as my rowing slowed slightly. "I'm not doing all the work here by myself."

Josh squinted ahead, holding on to the rudder with one hand as he used the other to shade his eyes from the bright morning sun, which was reflecting off the tiny waves all around us. "Can you guys see how deep the coral is up there?" he asked. "We need to find a low spot so we won't—"

He was interrupted by an ugly scraping sound. The raft suddenly slowed dramatically on my side, sort of like a giant hand had reached out and grabbed it. Or more accurately, a giant chunk of coral.

"We have to move left!" Josh shouted, dragging hard on the rudder. "We're going to go aground on the reef!"

The water was already getting choppy there around the reef, not as crystal clear as the water in the lagoon, but it was still clear enough to see the gnarled, cauliflower-

knobby shape of the coral, washed over in muted blues and reds. It looked sort of like the stuff that had grown on the egg salad I'd left in the fridge for a month, only larger and sharper.

Jabbing at the coral with my paddle, I tried to push the raft free of it. The first time, my makeshift oar skidded off to the side, almost crushing my fingers between the handle and the raft, but I immediately tried again. This time I found a good, solid spot from which to push off. There was another sickening scrape, but then, finally, the raft came loose again, bobbing up and down and drifting slowly counterclockwise.

"We did it!" Angela cried. "We're—"

The rest of her words were swallowed up in a giant splash as the first real ocean wave caught us, slapping down violently on the raft and shooting spray everywhere. The world seemed to go topsy-turvy for a few seconds while the raft careened sickeningly, spinning first in one direction and then another.

"Whoa!" Josh yelled, sounding nervous.

After that everything happened fast. Josh was shouting something else, but I couldn't hear it through the water in my ears. I dug frantically into the water with

my paddle, but it felt like rowing through mud. The current grabbed at the bottom of the paddle and yanked at it, as if there was some kind of huge, nasty mermaid down there playing tug-of-war with me.

"Dani!" Angela screeched. "Don't lean over so far! You'll tip us over!"

I opened my mouth to respond, but another wave roared over the raft at that moment, and I wound up almost choking on a faceful of salty sea water. The raft spun around and around until I wasn't sure which direction was which. The paddle was ripped out of my hands, which was just as well, because I needed both hands to grip the edge of the raft so I wouldn't be tossed headfirst into the reef. Splinters dug into my palms as I coughed, trying to expel the water I'd accidentally swallowed.

But despite my best efforts to hold on, I lost my grip on the raft. My eyes were squeezed shut, and I was already drenched from the spray, so it took me a moment or two to realize that I was underwater. In fact, it wasn't until I tried to breathe in a mouthful of salty water that I really figured it out.

I opened my eyes and found myself looking through

a murky haze that shimmered when I coughed. My lungs were burning, my hands were burning, and now my eyes were burning. Kicking my feet as hard as I could, hardly feeling the pain as they connected with sharp bits of the reef, I shot upward and bobbed to the surface just in time to see the raft—well, a largish chunk of it, anyway—sink out of sight beneath yet another wave. Gasping for breath, I coughed out about a gallon of water and spit, and then started sucking down the sweet, sweet air. The water was pretty choppy out there just beyond the reef, but I actually felt a little more secure treading water than I had on the raft. I'd grown up in Florida, so it wasn't like it was my first time in the ocean.

Shaking my wet hair out of my face, I glanced around for the others. Josh was treading water nearby. Angela was clinging to a small fragment of the raft that was still floating.

"Help! Help!" she shrieked, coughing dramatically as a wave washed over her.

Even under those circumstances, I couldn't help noticing that she didn't appear to be in any danger of

actually drowning. In fact, her hair was barely wet. Plus I happened to know that she'd been on the swim team at her neighborhood pool since second grade.

I guess Josh wasn't willing to take any chances, though. He swam over to her. "Don't panic, Angela," he cried. "You'll be okay. Just stick with me."

I would have rolled my eyes, but it would have taken too much effort. Instead I focused on trying to get myself back to shore while Josh paddled along nearby, doing the same for himself and the giant blond parasite that had attached herself to him. It took some pretty strong swimming to get past the reef without getting ourselves smashed against it, but we managed. Well, Josh and I managed. Angela pretty much just whimpered and allowed Josh to drag her along with him. Once we made it back to the calm waters of the lagoon, it was just a matter of swimming back to shore. The others, who had watched the whole disaster, waded out to help us to dry land.

So much for the King of Rafts. "The King is dead, long live the King," I muttered to myself as I collapsed onto the sand, feeling the burn of the coral cuts on my feet and the unpleasant itch of sand in my bathing suit.

Isle Be Seeing You

"Sorry, Josh," Chrissie said tentatively. "The raft looked really good for a while."

Josh sighed, looking haggard. "No, I'm the one who's sorry," he said, rubbing his head and making his wet hair stick up. "I really thought that slate rudder would be stronger, but it just snapped when we got out there in the rougher water. That's really why we got in trouble. Maybe if we rebuild, make the new rudder out of wood this time . . ."

At those words, I guess something inside of me snapped, just like the stupid rudder. Patience has never been my strongest virtue, so it was kind of amazing it hadn't happened sooner. "Are you nuts?" I exclaimed loudly.

Josh blinked at me. "Huh?"

"It wasn't just the rudder." Now that I'd gotten started, I couldn't seem to stop myself. My voice rose higher and higher, both in pitch and in volume, as I continued. "The raft was a total disaster. I knew it wasn't going to work from the beginning. I mean, who could possibly believe a bunch of twigs tied together is going to make it across two miles of ocean?" I glared at Josh, who just looked stunned.

"Shut up, Dani," Angela cried fervently. "Josh knows

what he's doing—that's why we elected him our leader. If he wants to rebuild, I think we should totally support him."

"Well, you can waste your time trying again if you want," I declared. "But I . . ."

My voice trailed off and my heart sank as Josh stood up, stared coldly at me, and stomped away without a word.

Eleven

I took a few steps after him, not sure whether to try to catch up and apologize. It wasn't that I was sorry about what I'd said, exactly. Now that it was out, I couldn't believe I'd ever kept it to myself for so long. But I knew I could have said it in a much nicer way.

"Nice going, McFeeney," Angela called sarcastically from behind me. "Very sensitive."

For once I didn't have a snappy response for her. I wandered a little farther down the beach, wondering exactly when I'd transformed into Tactfulina, Queen of the Big Mouths. Josh was still hurrying off along the beach, his hands shoved deep into his pockets and his head hanging low.

I chewed my lower lip as I drifted to a stop and watched him go. I was pretty certain that I'd just blown it once and for all. Why hadn't I stopped to think before going off on him like that? The least I could have done was take him off in private to tell him his idea stunk. Then again, we all know how that worked out last time. . . .

"Dani!" Kenny suddenly appeared at my side, panting and excited. He grabbed at my arm, accidentally scratching me with his fingernails. "C'mere!"

I yanked my arm free before he could draw blood. "Careful," I snapped. "What's wrong with you? Leave me alone."

"Come on!" he cried breathlessly, totally ignoring my testiness. "Macy and Ned are telling the others about our fire. They need your help to explain it!"

I sighed. "So much for keeping me out of it, like I asked," I muttered.

Still, at this point I figured I had nothing to lose by coming clean about my involvement with Kenny's plan.

Isle Be Seeing You

Especially since Getting the Heck Off This Stinking Island had just gone from #1 on my personal priority list to pretty much the *only* thing on the list. Kenny was already dashing back toward the rest of the group, and after one last glance at Josh's lonely figure, I turned and followed.

"Okay," Brooke was saying cautiously as I rejoined the group. "So this fire you built—it's up on the mountain, or what? How do you know it'll be visible way out there at sea?"

"Yeah." Cassie nodded, her eyes wide and worried. "Oh! And what if we set the whole island on fire by accident?"

"Hey, if the whole island was on fire, someone would definitely notice that!" Ryan joked.

Brooke rolled her eyes and frowned at him. "Be serious, Ryan," she scolded in her best fourteen-going-on-forty voice. "This is no time for your goofy jokes."

"Look, it's not going to set the island on fire, okay?" I spoke up. "Ned figured out exactly how to set it up so that wouldn't happen."

The others glanced at Ned, several of them nodding thoughtfully. Before the trip I was sure most of the people on the island—myself included—had thought of

Ned as little more than a TV-obsessed dweeb. That is, if we thought about him at all.

But we'd all learned that there was a lot more to him than that. For one thing he had a photographic memory for every obscure factoid he'd ever seen on TV or read on the Internet, which had made our lives on the island easier and saved our butts a time or two.

Despite their respect for Ned, though, the others still seemed a bit skeptical about the whole fire plan. I guess after just getting burned by the raft disaster, they were a bit cautious about throwing their energy and enthusiasm behind another plan.

As I was trying to figure out how to convince them to give it a chance, Ryan stepped forward. "Hey," he said, his voice more serious than usual. "If Dani thinks this plan will work—um, and Macy and Ned and Ken too—I think we should at least talk about it. Right?"

I shot him a quick, grateful smile. Even if it was only his crush talking, it was nice to have some support.

"I suppose." Brooke shrugged. "So let's—" She cut herself off. "Hi, Josh."

I jumped in surprise. Josh had returned so quietly that

Isle Be Seeing You

I hadn't even noticed him until Brooke said something. I stared at him so hard that it felt like my eyeballs would pop out of my head and tumble onto the sand. But he wasn't looking at me. He was sort of staring into space, his expression wavering somewhere between dejected and sheepish.

"What are you guys talking about?" he asked the group at large.

Macy, Ned, and I exchanged a quick, anxious look. I guess none of us was quite ready to speak up and tell him all about the plan we'd been concocting behind his back. Least of all me.

Luckily Kenny had no such qualms. "We're talking about a new plan," he said eagerly. "See, we figured out that if we could build a big, huge fire up on the ridge . . ." He went on, explaining the whole thing.

Josh nodded along, his expression slowly changing from downcast to interested. "Cool," he said when Kenny finished. "Let's do it."

I goggled at him. Was he serious? Did he really think the fire plan would work, or was he just eager to take the attention off what had just happened?

Castaways

Finally he glanced over at me, briefly meeting my eyes. But before I could figure out what he was thinking, Kenny let out a yelp.

"Hey!" he cried. "What time is it? We don't want to miss the boat!"

Everyone scrambled into action as we realized we didn't have much time. If that boat stayed true to schedule, it would be chugging into view of our island in less than an hour.

"Come on," Chrissie cried. "Let's get up to the ridge!"

We all took off down the beach. As we passed close to camp on our way to the trail, Ryan raced on ahead and woke up Mr. Truskey to tell him what was going on. "What's this I hear about a campfire, Counselor Bob?" the teacher burbled, staggering out of the shelter and grinning at us. He was dressed in a pair of jeans so dirty and raggedy that they would have made a scarecrow look underdressed, topped off with what appeared to be one of Kenny's T-shirts.

I grimaced, realizing that any rescue would come none too soon for Mr. Truskey. I just hoped his sanity was still in there somewhere.

But there was no time to ponder that at the moment.

Isle Be Seeing You

"Hurry," I panted, leading the way into the jungle.

We made it up to the ridge in record time. Well, all of us except for Mr. Truskey, who only followed along for about five minutes before getting distracted by a passing butterfly and wandered off in his own direction. As I emerged out of the cool mistiness of the jungle into the midmorning glare of the sunny clearing, I heard gasps and exclamations from the others and saw the amazed looks on their faces.

"Whoa," Ryan exclaimed. "This is going to be like *The Towering Inferno!*"

I guess the fire pile was sort of like a zit; if you see it every day you don't really notice exactly how much it's growing, even if you're aware that it's getting bigger. But now, looking at it through their eyes, I had to admit the pile really did look pretty impressive. Almost ten feet high, it first appeared to be nothing but a chaotic jumble of jungle junk. However, upon closer inspection it became possible to see that it was arranged in a definite pattern, an intricate crisscrossing network of layers, each one built upon the next. If you took away any of the large branches, or one soft nest of dry leaves, the whole thing would be a mess. But as it was, it was perfect.

Castaways

"Wow." Josh let out a long whistle. "You guys have really been working on this!"

Ned looked shy yet proud. And no wonder—the whole thing was thanks to him. Without his input the fire pile would have been just that. A pile, nothing more.

"Yeah," he said. "Um, thanks. We all worked pretty hard."

"It was my idea!" Kenny spoke up, puffing out his skinny little chest proudly.

Ned laughed. "Yep," he agreed. "You were the master-mind, Ken." He reached into his shorts pocket and pulled out a book of matches. "So Josh, you're the leader—want to light it?"

Josh pushed away the matches. "No way, dude," he said with a smile. "It's all you. You do the honors."

"Yeah, go for it, Ned," Brooke said.

"Whoo-hoo, Ned!" Chrissie sang out. "You the man!"

"You the man, you the man!" Kenny repeated happily.

Macy smiled at Ned. "Go ahead. Light it."

"Well . . . okay." Ned looked abashed by all the sudden attention. He flipped open the matchbook, revealing that there were only half a dozen matches left inside. "Um, here goes."

"Hey, I feel like we should make a little speech or something," I joked, feeling a little excited in spite of my worries. "Like, hereby we dedicate this fire to the castaway within all of us. . . ."

Angela snorted. "Grow up, Dani."

But the others seemed to catch my spirit of silliness. "And we send forth this smoke to carry our voices to the world." Josh picked up where I'd left off. "And to express our desires to be rescued and returned to our homes. . . ."

"With liberty and justice for all," Brooke added in a rather pompous tone.

That did it. Ryan started to laugh, and Kenny joined in. Soon the twins dissolved into giggles, and before long, everyone else was laughing too. Brooke tried to look insulted for a moment, but finally she grinned.

"Okay, okay," she cried over the laughter. "Go on, Ned. Let's get this sucker burning already!"

We all cheered loudly. Ned scratched one of the matches across the igniter strip, and it flickered into life. "Here goes nothing," he said.

Leaning forward, he touched the flame to a slender twig jutting out from the pile and carefully retrieved

it. Moving quickly around the perimeter of the pile, he lit as many twigs as he could before the burning piece of kindling threatened his fingers.

Then he flicked the still-burning twig into the pile. "Okay, everyone should probably move back a little," he suggested, already moving to follow his own advice. "If this thing burns like it's supposed to, it'll get pretty hot pretty fast."

We all stepped back to the edge of the clearing, our eyes trained on the tiny, sputtering flames as they struggled to stay alive in the breeze. I held my breath, hardly daring to hope that the fire pile would work.

It worked. Those first tiny flames ate their way along their twigs to a thick layer of dry leaves and other kindling, which began to smolder and then burn more vigorously. Soon the fire was crackling along the edges of the larger branches, and after that it was like a chain reaction, each layer of flame spreading upward and downward to ignite the rest of the pile. Before long the whole thing was aflame, crackling away loudly and sending great quantities of smoke pouring up into the air. It was a pretty impressive sight; if I hadn't known better, I would have thought it was a volcano erupting. Of course,

if that had been the case, I knew of a certain blond-haired girly-girl we would have been able to sacrifice to the volcano spirits. . . .

"Excellent!" Josh's eyes were trained on the smoke, which drifted and spread across the sky like huge gray tentacles.

I coughed as a sudden breeze carried some of the smoke directly into my face. "Yeah, awesome job, Ned," I choked out between coughs.

Ned hardly seemed to hear the compliments. He was peering through the dense smoke toward the horizon. "The boat should be here any second now. . . ."

Grabbing Macy's wrist and checking her watch, I saw that he was right. I don't know about anyone else, but I hardly breathed for the next few moments as we all waited. My eyes were watering from the smoke, but I kept them wide open as I stared out to sea.

Finally Kenny let out an excited shriek. "There it is!" he cried, jumping up and down and jabbing his finger toward the horizon.

"I see it! I see it!" Cassie sounded so excited I was afraid she might start hyperventilating.

Everyone started jabbering at once, laughing and screaming and jumping up and down. "Wait!" I yelled above the clamor. "Chill out, okay? We don't even know if they'll see us."

"Way to be optimistic, Dani." Angela rolled her eyes.

But they all kept quiet for the next few minutes . . . as the boat chugged right on past and disappeared from sight again. I went limp, as if someone had just turned all my bones to Jell-O. So much for that.

"Don't worry." I could tell Ryan was trying to sound cheerful. "Even if they didn't notice the smoke, the people on that other island probably will."

"Yeah," Brooke agreed, though she didn't sound cheerful at all. "Anyway, we can try again tomorrow. I guess."

"How?" Angela was still staring out at the empty horizon. "There's no way we can get together another huge pile like this in one day. Not even with all of us working on it this time."

"So maybe it won't take one day." Macy's voice was quiet but determined. "We still have to keep trying."

I just sighed, not too sure about that myself. But I kept quiet as they started debating about what to do. After all the drama, the ups and downs of the past few days, I was suddenly just too exhausted to argue or plan or think anymore.

Isle Be Seeing You

Josh stepped toward me, his face somber. "Can I talk to you for a minute?"

My stomach clenched nervously. "Sure."

We slipped away from the group, moving around behind a rocky outcropping near the edge of the jungle. It was only about chest-high, which meant we were still within sight of the others, but it was far enough away to give us a little privacy as long as we kept our voices down.

"Listen." Josh took a deep breath. "I just wanted to apologize. You know—for before."

"What?" For a moment I was confused. "You mean the raft? That's okay, there's no way you—"

"Not the raft," he cut me off. "After that. I kind of acted like a baby. You know, when you said the raft was a total disaster."

I winced at hearing my own words again. "No, I'm the one who should say I'm sorry. I was totally rude."

"That's okay. Anyway, you were right. The raft *was* a disaster; I should've realized that sooner. This was a much better idea." He waved one hand in the direction of the fire. "So how come you didn't tell me about it sooner?"

I didn't really have an answer for that, so I just

shrugged. "So what does this mean?" I asked tentatively. "You know—for us."

"What do you mean?" Suddenly Josh looked uncomfortable. "I thought we already talked about that. You know."

I wasn't sure I did. "But are we still . . ." I swallowed hard, realizing I might be heading into territory I didn't really want to visit. Then again, wasn't it better to get it out in the open? "Like, at first I sort of understood why you wanted to keep things a secret. You know—about us. At least I thought I did. But then I started to wonder if, well, you weren't really sure about the whole thing, and that's why—"

"Hey!" Kenny's shout interrupted whatever I was trying to say, which was just as well, since I wasn't too sure it was coming out right. "Check it out! The boat! It's coming back!"

Josh and I both gasped. "Really?" Josh cried, hurrying back around the outcroppping. The others were staring off toward the horizon, babbling in confusion and/or excitement.

I followed Josh around the rocks, already squinting in the same direction as everyone else. "Where?" I demanded. "I can't see anything through all this smoke."

"There!" Josh pointed. "Look, Kenny's right! The boat's coming back!"

I finally saw it then too. The boat was chug-chugging along in the opposite direction from its usual path. As I stared, hardly daring to believe my eyes, a tiny pinprick of reddish brightness sailed up into the air, arcing over its decks.

"A flare!" Ryan shrieked. "They're setting off a flare! They see us! They see us!"

"They see us! They see us!" Cassie chanted.

Josh laughed out loud. "They see us," he repeated in amazement. Turning to stare at me, he grinned. "They see us!"

Before I quite knew what was happening, he threw his arms around me and planted a big, juicy kiss right on my lips. I kissed him back, open-eyed and smiling, so startled and happy at first that I couldn't focus on anything else.

Then my gaze shifted slightly, and I saw something that made me even happier. Angela was staring right at us, her mouth hanging open in shock and horror.

Twelve

"Ugh," Michelle groaned as she slammed her locker door shut. "I can't believe I totally forgot to study for my English quiz."

I grinned at her. "Bummer and a half," I said. "Guess you were too busy studying for that math quiz you flunked yesterday."

"Nice." Michelle rolled her eyes. "Good to know I have the sympathy of my best friends. Not."

We entered the stream of students pouring down the hall. Tina was walking on my other side. "So tomorrow's

Friday, guys," she said. "Want to hit the mall this weekend? My sister said she'd drive us."

"I'm in," I said immediately.

It felt good to think about quizzes and shopping rather than hauling water or cracking open coconuts. It was only a little over a week since we'd been rescued from the island, and it was kind of surprising how most of my life was already totally back to normal. For the first few days I'd felt like some kind of celebrity—everyone at school and in our hometown had wanted to talk to us about being stuck on the island for so long. A bunch of TV news teams and newspaper reporters from nearby cities turned up to talk to us, and we even did a satellite interview with one of the national morning shows from New York. That was pretty cool, even though Angela managed to plop herself right in the front row and hog most of the camera time.

Anyway, all the attention faded almost as quickly as my sunburn. Within a few days other things happened, and people started to lose interest in hearing our story for the fifteenth time. My parents were still being extra nice to me and Kenny, but otherwise it was almost as if we'd never been gone.

Castaways

Well, almost. I peeled off from my friends when we reached the entrance to the science wing. As I headed toward my classroom I spotted Macy walking toward a different room. She passed by that way every day on her way to Ms. Watson's class, though before Castaway Island I'd never really noticed her. Now I would have noticed her anyway, but it was especially hard to miss her since she was usually walking with her new friend, Brooke. Somehow I'd missed noticing that the two of them were hanging out a lot on the island.

They smiled, waving at me. I returned the wave, noticing that Macy's clothes were back to looking like she was one step away from being Amish. But there was something different about her these days, something quite separate from her looks. I guess it was extra confidence or something. I don't know, I'm not a psychologist or anything, but I sort of think our time on the island might actually have been good for her.

I slid into Mr. Truskey's classroom a split second before the late bell rang. Oh, right, Mr. Truskey—I almost forgot to mention that he was pretty much back to normal, too. Well, as normal as he'd ever been, anyway; in other words, only moderately crazy rather than off-his-rocker nuts. He'd spent a couple of days in the hospital, where they'd treated his blood with some kind of new cutting-edge treatment to remove the last remnants of choo-choo goo from his body. The details were a little unclear, though he claimed we were going to be doing a unit about it at the end of the semester if we had enough time. Yeah. I was really looking forward to that.

As I dropped my books on my desk, I saw that Ryan was capering in front of Cassie's seat while she giggled delightedly at his antics. If Macy and Brooke seemed like an odd pair, then Ryan and Cassie? Totally bizarre. But I guess as soon as Ryan realized I was out of the picture—which he handled with surprising maturity, by the way, especially considering how idiotically I'd handled the whole situation—he noticed that one of the cutest girls in school was right there giggling at every one of his goofy jokes. It was pretty strange to think that if we'd never been stranded, the two of them probably never would have realized they liked each other. I guess it was strange for poor Chrissie, too. She tended to stare at her twin these days as if she'd suddenly started dating a space alien.

Speaking of creatures from other planets, Mr. Truskey strode into the room at that moment. He was dressed in

his daily uniform of jeans, a T-shirt, and flip-flops. His shirt sported a slightly faded picture of a tree and the words "Plants are people too." For Mr. T, our time as castaways had been just one more entry on his long list of adventures. Probably not even the weirdest one he'd had that decade.

"Listen up, people!" he cried, waving his arms over his head. "We have a lot of ground to cover today. . . ."

I tuned out as he started in on one of his rambling lectures about biodiversity or bioethics or bio-something-or-other. Watching him pace back and forth at the front of the room, his wild black hair sticking up, his brown eyes wide with enthusiasm, and his flip-flops flapping against the tile floor, it would be pretty easy to believe that the trip had never happened at all. That I'd just fallen asleep during class and dreamed the whole thing.

But I knew that couldn't be true. Mr. Truskey aside, too much had changed. Brooke had stepped back enough from being Miss Everything Must Be Perfect to realize that she could have a friend like Macy. Macy had overcome her shyness enough to accept that friendship. Cassie had possibly suffered some kind of brain hemorrhage or mosquito-borne dementia that

made her think Ryan was cute. Well, okay, maybe that's kind of mean. But something had changed in both her and Ryan, at least a little, or their new relationship wouldn't have lasted past the trip home.

I thought about all that a bit more as Mr. Truskey's voice droned away in the background. Not only had most of the people from the island changed inside themselves, but my opinion of them had changed. I'd always considered Cassie and Chrissie friends, of course, but the others? Not so much. Yet now, even if I wasn't planning on spending much time discussing student government issues with Brooke or hanging out at Ned's house watching TV, I knew we were all sort of bonded by what we'd gone through together. Kind of like brothers and sisters or something.

Speaking of which, one of the biggest changes of all had to be me and Kenny. I guess it took being stranded on an island with him for me to realize that my little brother was actually sort of a cool person underneath the sniffles and the bugs and all the rest of it. I don't know why it took me so long to see that—after all, he was related to me! All I know is that my parents just about had a heart attack on our first night home when I actually apologized to him—without them forcing me to—after I accidentally called him a dorky little loser. Hey, old habits are hard to break.

We'd sort of slid back into some of those old habits since then, and we were back to arguing and name-calling most of the time. But I was careful now not to be quite so mean to him, and I think he was trying not to be quite so obnoxious to me. He'd even confessed to voting for Angela in that election for island leader way back at the beginning, though he said he'd only done it to make me mad.

Which meant, of course, that my last lingering, anxious question had been answered. Josh had voted for me.

I smiled dreamily as I thought about Josh. Things between us were better than ever, now that everything was out in the open. Not that I didn't still have my moments of doubt about the whole shebang, especially when I caught myself doing something girly like writing his initials in my notebook or taking extra time picking out my clothes in the morning. But I was trying to cut myself some slack on that. It wasn't every day that a girl had her first boyfriend, and I wanted to enjoy it.

Anyway, Josh admitted now that it had been stupid to try to keep things a secret. He said he just wasn't sure

how to handle it, and he figured it would be easier that way. That made me realize that he wasn't quite as perfect as he always seemed—he was just better at hiding it than most people. And somehow, knowing that he wasn't perfect only made me like him more.

Speaking of allegedly perfect people . . . As Mr. Truskey started scribbling on the board, my mind wandered back to that delicious, delightful moment when Angela had first realized that Josh and I were a couple. She was so freaked out about it that she didn't say a single word to either of us during the entire trip back to the mainland and then home again. Since we'd been back at school, she hadn't spoken to me or voluntarily come within about five feet. Not that that was so unusual or anything.

When the bell finally rang to release us from Mr. Truskey's class, I was the first one out the door. It was lunchtime, which was the only time I got to hang out with Josh all day. That was the one bad thing about going with a seventh grader—we didn't have a single class together. But he'd started sitting with me and my friends on our first day back, and by now it almost felt like it had always been that way.

I was halfway down the hall when Angela stepped out

in front of me. I put on the brakes, planning to dodge her and keep going.

"Hey, Dani," she called out. "Hold up."

I skidded to a halt so fast that if I'd been a cartoon character my tracks would be smoking. "Huh?"

Angela reached out and grabbed my arm just above the elbow. I stared down at her hand, too confused to react. As far as I could recall, Angela had never actually touched me before. Well, not unless you counted the time she'd kicked me in the shins back in second grade. Or the time a year or two later when she'd pinched me hard enough to leave a bruise. Or—

"Come on," she commanded impatiently, interrupting my little trip down Memories-of-Evil Lane. "I want to talk to you. Over here."

Still a little in shock, I allowed her to drag me off to a quiet spot behind the water fountain. She dropped my arm and turned to face me, taking a deep breath. I braced myself, preparing for whatever new level of evil she had in mind.

"Look," she said. "I just wanted to say, like, good for you. You know, for getting together with Josh. That's kind of cool, you know?"

Isle Be Seeing You

I was astonished. Was this just the setup for some kind of dastardly plan, or had Angela Barnes actually just . . . congratulated me?

"Um . . . ," I said blankly.

"Anyway," she continued, "I was sort of annoyed about it at first. . . ."

Yeah. Sort of annoyed the way the United States was sort of annoyed after the attack on Pearl Harbor.

"But then I thought about it, and now I think you're kind of a cute couple," she finished.

I smiled cautiously, waiting for the punchline. When none seemed forthcoming, I ventured a response. "Oh," I said.

Angela stared at me. "By the way, you have something stuck in your teeth," she said with a ghost of a smirk. "Did you have, like, spinach or something for breakfast?"

With that, she strode off down the hall, quickly becoming lost in the crowds of kids pushing and shoving their way toward the cafeteria. Picking absentmindedly at my teeth, I headed in that direction myself.

"What was that all about?" I muttered.

At first I speculated about various complex and reprehensible plots to make me look stupid. But then I realized

the truth might be simpler than that—but much, much stranger to contemplate. Could it be that Angela was a little bit nicer than I'd thought? Or at least not completely, utterly, and irredeemably evil?

It was a bizarre thought. Even if it was true, I was pretty sure that Not-So-Evil Angela and I weren't about to suddenly become the best of pals or anything. But maybe we'd both learned something about each other during our time on the island together.

That didn't seem so strange. After all, I knew I'd certainly learned a lot about myself. For instance, I'd learned that it was possible and even sort of okay for me to act like a girly-girl sometimes, just as long as it didn't stop me from being true to myself and speaking my mind. See, I'd finally realized that was exactly what a good girlfriend should do—speak up and say what she was thinking, even if she wasn't sure it was what the other person wanted to hear. If I'd done that in the first place, maybe we would have skipped the raft fiasco and been rescued earlier.

Anyway, I guess it was true that being castaways had changed all of us. Maybe even Evil Angela Barnes.

Just then I turned the corner at the end of the hall and

spotted Josh waiting for me outside the cafeteria doors. His whole face broke into a huge grin when he saw me, and he lifted one hand in a casual sort of wave. I waved back, dodging around a little cluster of people in my way. It wasn't until I heard a certain high-pitched, familiar, totally girly giggle that I realized one of those people was Angela. Glancing over, I saw her fluttering her eyelashes at the trio of cute seventh-grade boys surrounding her.

I rolled my eyes. Then again, some things never change.

The End

star
by Catherin Hapka

power

She's beautiful, she's talented, she's famous.

She's a star!

Things would be perfect
if only her family
was around to help
her celebrate. . . .

Follow the
adventures of
fourteen-year-old
pop star
Star Calloway

She's sharp.

She's smart.

She's confident.

She's unstoppable.

And she's on your trail.

MEET THE NEW NANCY DREW

Still sleuthing,

still solving crimes,

but she's got some new tricks up her sleeve!

NANCY DREW

girl detective

HAVE YOU READ ALL OF THE ALICE BOOKS?

PHYLLIS REYNOLDS NAYLOR

STARTING WITH ALICE
Atheneum Books for
  Young Readers
  0-689-84395-X
Aladdin Paperbacks
  0-689-84396-8

ALICE IN BLUNDERLAND
Atheneum Books for
  Young Readers
  0-689-84397-6

LOVINGLY ALICE
Atheneum Books for
  Young Readers
  0-689-84399-2

THE AGONY OF ALICE
Atheneum Books for
  Young Readers
  0-689-31143-5
Aladdin Paperbacks
  0-689-81672-3

ALICE IN RAPTURE,
  SORT-OF
Atheneum Books for
  Young Readers
  0-689-31466-3
Aladdin Paperbacks
  0-689-81687-1

RELUCTANTLY ALICE
Atheneum Books for
  Young Readers
  0-689-31681-X
Aladdin Paperbacks
  0-689-81688-X

ALL BUT ALICE
Atheneum Books for
Young Readers
  0-689-31773-5
Aladdin Paperbacks
  0-689-85044-1

ALICE IN APRIL
Atheneum Books for
  Young Readers
  0-689-31805-7
Aladdin Paperbacks
  0-689-81686-3

ALICE IN-BETWEEN
Atheneum Books for
  Young Readers
  0-689-31890-0
Aladdin Paperbacks
  0-689-81685-5

ALICE THE BRAVE
Atheneum Books for
  Young Readers
  0-689-80095-9
Aladdin Paperbacks
  0-689-80598-5

ALICE IN LACE
Atheneum Books for
  Young Readers
  0-689-80358-3
Aladdin Paperbacks
  0-689-80597-7

OUTRAGEOUSLY ALICE
Atheneum Books for
  Young Readers
  0-689-80354-0
Aladdin Paperbacks
  0-689-80596-9

ACHINGLY ALICE
Atheneum Books for
  Young Readers
  0-689-80533-9
Aladdin Paperbacks
  0-689-80595-0
Simon Pulse
  0-689-86396-9

ALICE ON THE OUTSIDE
Atheneum Books for
  Young Readers
  0-689-80359-1
Simon Pulse
  0-689-80594-2

GROOMING OF ALICE
Atheneum Books for
  Young Readers
  0-689-82633-8
Simon Pulse
  0-689-84618-5

ALICE ALONE
Atheneum Books for
  Young Readers
  0-689-82634-6
Simon Pulse
  0-689-85189-8

SIMPLY ALICE
Atheneum Books for
  Young Readers
  0-689-84751-3
Simon Pulse
  0-689-85965-1

PATIENTLY ALICE
Atheneum Books for
  Young Readers
  0-689-82636-2
Simon Pulse
  0-689-87073-6

INCLUDING ALICE
Atheneum Books for
  Young Readers
  0-689-82637-0

Step back in time with Warren and Betsy through the power of the Instant Commuter invention and relive, in exciting detail, the greatest natural disasters of all time. . . .

PEG KEHRET

THE VOLCANO DISASTER

Visit the great volcano eruption of Mount St. Helens, in Washington, on May 18, 1980. . . .

"Touching on some interesting problems in time travel, this fast-paced novel combines elements of fantasy with a disaster story. . . . A bibliography of books on volcanoes is appended."—*Booklist*

Florida Sunshine State Award Winner

THE BLIZZARD DISASTER

Try to survive the terrifying blizzard of November 11, 1940, in Minnesota. . . .

"Intriguing . . . high level of suspense. . . . Scenes described with chilling accuracy and the characters' emotional reactions are both realistic and moving."—*School Library Jounal*

"Science and historical fiction blend. . . . The resourceful kids [are] researchers [who] have material for a wonderful narrative report. . . . Fast paced and exciting."—*Booklist*

Iowa Children's Choice Master List 2000/2001

THE FLOOD DISASTER

Can they return to the past in time to save lives?

Iowa Children's Choice Award Master List 2000/2001

Available from Simon & Schuster

The Newbery Medal is awarded each year to the most distinguished contribution to literature for children published in the U.S. How many of these Newbery winners, available from Aladdin and Simon Pulse, have you read?

NEWBERY MEDAL WINNERS

❏ *King of the Wind*
by Marguerite Henry
0-689-71486-6

❏ *M.C. Higgins, the Great*
by Virginia Hamilton
0-02-043490-1

❏ *Caddie Woodlawn*
by Carol Ryrie Brink
0-689-81521-2

❏ *Call It Courage*
by Armstrong Sperry
0-02-045270-5

❏ *The Cat Who Went
to Heaven*
by Elizabeth Coatsworth
0-698-71433-5

❏ *From the Mixed-up
Files of Mrs. Basil E.
Frankweiler*
by E. L. Konigsburg
0-689-71181-6

❏ *A Gathering of Days*
by Joan W. Blos
0-689-71419-X

❏ *The Grey King*
by Susan Cooper
0-689-71089-5

❏ *Hitty: Her First
Hundred Years*
by Rachel Field
0-689-82284-7

❏ *Mrs. Frisby and the
Rats of NIMH*
by Robert C. O'Brien
0-689-71068-2

❏ *Shadow of a Bull*
by Maia Wojciechowska
0-689-71567-6

❏ *Smoky the Cow
Horse*
by Eric P. Kelly
0-689-71682-6

❏ *The View from
Saturday*
by E. L. Konigsburg
0-689-81721-5

❏ *Dicey's Song*
by Cynthia Voigt
0-689-81721-5